DRESSING

THE

SAINTS

DRESSING
THE
SAINTS

Aracelis González Asendorf

BLACK LAWRENCE PRESS

Black Lawrence Press

Executive Editor: Diane Goettel
Cover Artwork: "Azure" by Erika Masterson
Cover Design: Zoe Norvell
Interior Design: www.ineedabookinterior.com

Published 2024 by Black Lawrence Press.
Printed in the United States.

IN MEMORY OF MIS QUERIDOS PADRES,
NOEL GONZÁLEZ Y ARACELIS GONZÁLEZ
AND MY BELOVED HUSBAND,
ALAN ASENDORF
I CARRY YOU IN MY HEART.

FOR MY CHILDREN,
ALEXA AND CORD

Table of Contents

THE LOST ONES

Efraín hadn't been out all day. He didn't really need anything from la bodeguita, but the house smelled like dirty, wet socks,
and it would for the next couple of hours, until the dust burned off
the coils. It happened every year the first time the central heat was
turned on for the winter. Now the sour, musty smell combined with
Emelina's cigarette smoke, and Efraín had to leave.

"Emelina, I'm driving to la bodeguita," he said to his wife who
sat in a flannel robe watching television, her once-blue slippers
propped on the coffee table. "Did you hear me, Eme?" Emelina
didn't look away from the set. She tilted her chin up to exhale, and
the details of her face were lost in a haze of gray. He knew he was
wasting his words on the woman he'd met smoking behind a stand
of palmettos forty-five years ago, but he added, "You shouldn't
smoke inside the house. You shouldn't smoke at all."

Emelina looked at him and blew two perfect smoke rings his
way.

Efraín shook his head and shifted his weight from his weak foot to his strong one. Housebound after the roofing accident, he now knew Eme's afternoon routine. This was one of the four Newport cigarettes his wife allowed herself each day. After coming home from St. Anthony's Elementary school where she worked as a kindergarten aide, she changed out of her work clothes and sat in front of the TV placing her cigarettes single file, yellow filter tips uniformly aligned, on the coffee table. She smoked two while she watched Ellen, and two during that idiot Dr. Phil. Then, she showered and made dinner. That's when he would arrive home from work before his accident, when Eme had dinner ready. He hadn't known that she even had a routine until three months ago when he'd fallen and shattered his ankle. He was inspecting work completed by the crew of the small company he owned when the edge of his foot caught an upraised shingle sending him, shocked and spiraling, down the length of the steep-pitched roof.

Fell off a goddamn roof after spending the better part of my life roofing.

That's what he said to people who asked, more curious than concerned, at la bodeguita. Of course, it wasn't really a bodeguita at all; not like the little stores in West Tampa stocked with Cuban products, smelling of root vegetables, cumin, and dry-salted cod. This one, barely a mile from his house, was just a regular mini-mart: gas pumps, beer, bad coffee, pre-fab sandwiches, and lottery tickets.

Still, it offered a break from the house and Eme's smoking.

Efraín had always disliked Emelina's cigarettes, but her smoke, blended with the smell from the air system, made the house even more unbearable that afternoon than it had been during the last three months. Emelina tended to him dutifully following the accident, just as he had cared for her years ago during her pérdidas. That's what they came to call her repeated miscarriages over the years. Her pérdidas. But while he had given his attention generously during her losses, he felt Emelina was miserly with hers. She was impatient as she helped him out of bed and to the bathroom. She was brusque in manner as she settled him on the couch in front of the television or helped him bathe; the ordinary necessities of the day. It humiliated him to need help.

"You can leave," he said to her a week after the accident, more out of disappointment and weariness than anger. "Go back to work. I don't need you to stay."

Emelina was visibly relieved to return to her job and the children, and he made do alone. Efraín had to admit he envied her the distraction of work. Without it he felt lost. Without it he felt the way he did as a boy standing on the tarmac of the Miami airport with nothing but a small suitcase and a name tag.

Outside, the chilly dampness of the afternoon startled his body as if he'd been dunked in icy water, and it wasn't even all that cold yet. Not really. Not Nebraska cold. It was the first day the Florida temperatures had significantly dropped for the season, and they'd continue to fall as day turned into night. Efraín hated winter. He hated the way the cold seemed to find him once it started, creeping up his sleeves and down his collar, pinching his ears and smarting his eyes no matter what he did to guard himself against it. And this winter brought with it a previously unknown discomfort, a constant ache from the pins that now held his ankle together.

Efraín started his truck and waited for the engine to heat up. He waited for warm air to blow from the vents, and when it did, he rubbed his hands in front of them as if in front of a fire. He figured he'd go get his weekly lotto, and get away from Emelina and her afternoon cigarettes as the house warmed up.

Emelina had been smoking the first time Efraín met her, back in 1966. It had been at a get-together at his friend Rafaelito's house, and he'd only been in Tampa a few weeks. He'd gone to the back yard, away from the noisy chatter of the house, to the end of the property where a stand of palmettos grew. He found Emelina behind them. She wore a short navy-blue dress with a white sailor collar and stood there in white high-heeled sandals with perfectly polished coral toenails, holding a cigarette with the tips of her outstretched fingers.

You caught me," she said, adding quickly, "Papi doesn't approve."

He mumbled something apologetic, and turned to leave, but she stopped him.

"When did you get here?"

He knew by the way she said *here*, that she didn't mean here as in the backyard, or even here as in Tampa, but here as in the United States.

"Over three years ago," he said, "Pedro Pan. You?"

"Just this past year. Camarioca Boatlift. Directo a Tampa?"

He shook his head, "Nebraska."

"Nebraska? Where is that?" Emelina asked.

The truck warmed up during the brief drive to the mini-mart, but the steering wheel felt thick and cold in Efraín's hands, and the chill of the vinyl seats made its way through his clothes. As he pulled into the mini-mart, feeling his pockets for his cell phone, his attention was drawn to an ordinary woman by the notice of two unremarkable things. She'd gotten out of a taxi, an unusual sight in this suburban part of town where everyone drove themselves; and, even though he couldn't hear her, he knew by her body language that she was speaking Spanish. She touched her heart with one palm, and held up the other flat, patting the air before her, shaking her head and scrunching her shoulders all in one simultaneous motion.

Efraín parked and rummaged in the glove compartment for his penciled lotto play slip. He finally found it beneath some paper napkins he'd carelessly tossed in a few days before. The slip was worn and dog-eared; he needed to fill out a new one.

"Why don't you buy Advance Play?" Emelina asked him once, "you play the same numbers every week; just buy the same ticket weeks ahead without the bother."

"Because," Efraín said, "it would be like spitting in the face of fate."

"Do you believe in fate?" Eme asked.

Efraín wasn't sure. If he hadn't met Rafaelito he wouldn't have come to Tampa, and he wouldn't have met Eme. He wouldn't have started roofing and broken his ankle. Was that fate?

In the parking lot of the mini-mart, Efraín kept the truck motor running, and enjoyed the blast of warm air. He used the center of the steering wheel as a table top, carefully penciling in his numbers on a crisp play slip. The knock on his door window startled him. It was the woman from the taxi.

He rolled down the glass and cold air invaded his truck.

"Habla español?" the woman asked him.

Efraín nodded.

"Mire," the woman started. She said el chofer, el taxista, had brought her here from the bus terminal, but she didn't think this was the address, and she didn't understand anything he'd said. He'd driven her back and forth, she said pointing to the road that fronted the mini-mart, and then made her get out of the cab.

Efraín looked at the woman, trying hard to follow what she

said. He had no trouble with Spanish, even though his conversations with Emelina usually fell into English, and he'd stopped thinking in his native language God knew how many years ago. He still spoke rapidly his Cuban Spanish with swallowed final syllables and non-existent plural S's. He spoke effortlessly with Puerto Ricans who couldn't roll R's, and emphasized everything with bendito this, and bendito that. But this woman's Spanish was clipped, yet lilting, rising and falling in a cadence that left him wondering if she was asking a question or making a statement.

She stood there, pushing stray strands of hair away from her weathered face, clutching a piece of paper, telling him she was lost.

"Tell me what your paper says," Efraín said.

"No puedo," she responded.

"Why can't you?"

"Because I can't."

Efraín looked at the woman, realizing she didn't know how to read, and said softly, "Por favor, señora, let me see."

He looked at the scribbled address on the wrinkled paper, a Fletcher Avenue address, the road behind him. He glanced over his shoulder, the east-west artery already filling with rush hour traffic, and saw the taxi pull away. He looked down from the truck at the woman. She was squat and round, wearing gray sweatpants and an oversized men's jacket. Efraín sighed, half in pity, half in resignation, and asked her to get in the truck.

She climbed in with a knapsack and a small brown duffle. He began to say she could put them in the flatbed, but she put them on the floor in front of her and placed her feet carefully on top of them. Efraín noticed the side of her black sneaker was taped with a silver strip of frayed duct tape. A doughy smell of corn tamales emanated from her knapsack.

Efraín studied the address as she explained she was trying to find her brother.

"Where are you coming from?" Efraín asked.

"Carolina del Norte," she said. "I came for the strawberries." The strawberries were ripening and picking season would begin soon on the east side of the county. Harvesting work would be plentiful.

"It is very early for them," she sang, "but, well, usted sabe, la Migra."

Efraín stuck his play slip over the visor and backed towards Fletcher Avenue. He believed from the numbers on the address that it shouldn't be far, just slightly west of the mini-mart. He waited for a break in traffic, as the afternoon crawl began.

"Gracias, señor," she said.

Efraín shrugged a de nada as they waited for a red light to change.

She rubbed her hands in front of the air vent as he had done earlier, and asked politely, "What is your country?"

"Cuba," he said.

"How long have you been here?" she asked. "Hace mucho tiempo?"

"Sí," Efraín nodded, "it has been a very long time."

"Desde cuándo, señor?"

"1962."

Efraín was fourteen. Fidel had closed private schools and formed youth patrols; young teenagers were being sent into the interior to work on agricultural farms and teach illiterate campesinos to read. They can't get their hands on him; he heard his mother tell his father one night.

Efraín inched his truck along with traffic, west towards the sinking sun. The woman rearranged her feet around her belongings. She lowered the top of her jacket zipper just slightly where it had been pressing against her chin. He realized it made it more comfortable for her to breathe and speak as she repeated his words back to him.

"It has been a very long time," she said. "You came with your family, no?"

Efraín darted his eyes back and forth repeatedly from the wrinkled paper in his hand to the red brake lights of the car in front of him as if that would wipe away the images of the day he left Havana and his family.

"Señora, I believe the address is not far from here," he said, his voice tight and strained, although there was no zipper pressing against his chin.

Pedro Pan. Efraín remembered standing on the tarmac of the Miami airport, wearing a name tag and feeling lost. Many children, some so young they clutched a stuffed animal or doll, were met by relatives. Others, like him, were placed on a bus and driven to Camp Matecumbe, a processing center.

That's where he first met Rafaelito; he too, was alone. Two weeks later, with no word from his parents, he boarded another bus, together with Rafaelito. This time they were escorted by a young nun from Catholic Family Services, who rode with them to a boys' home in Nebraska.

The longer Efraín rode on the bus, the colder the weather became. The monjita spoke to him cheerfully. He knew it was cheerfully because she smiled and patted his hand, but he couldn't understand a word she said. She even said his name wrong, *Efren*, as if it had no a or i.

Efraín felt a sudden chill as he drove cautiously in the stop-and-go traffic looking for the address on the worn sheet of paper. Suddenly the numbers were too low, and he cursed silently, assuming he'd missed it and doubling back. It happened again; a ten-number jump. There was an entrance to a condo complex where the number he searched for should be, and Efraín knew it wasn't the place, but he turned in anyway. It was a gated complex that didn't allow passage past the main driveway without an entry code. He turned the truck around, pulling along the length of a white-painted curb.

Did she have a phone number, he asked? Was she certain of the address, was her brother waiting? Bueno, she said and explained. Her brother expected her for the strawberries, he'd given the address over a pay phone to someone she knew. When word spread through North Carolina that la Migra was tightening down, she decided to leave early. She presented the address at the bus terminal and bought a ticket. She couldn't read, she said apologetically. But, she added proudly, she could count.

Efraín leaned towards the steering wheel and back again, shifting around in his seat; God, he hated buses.

At the boys' home in Nebraska he bunked with Rafaelito. They were the same age. After lights out they traded stories about their families and homes as they boasted of baseball feats, carefully avoiding with false bravado how scared and lonely they were. They started to crunch English words out of their mouths as they awaited letters from home.

They hoped to be reunited soon, the letters said, although the ones from Efraín's mother contained no specifics. Ten months later, as if a present for his fifteenth birthday, Rafaelito received a telegram saying his family was in Florida. Efraín began writing home every day. When are you coming? He asked in every letter.

Things were uncertain, his mother wrote back. His father wasn't sure when they could leave. Her letters became repetitious as Efraín turned sixteen, seventeen, and then could see eighteen. The sprawling house of his boyhood, in the elegant Vedado neighborhood of Havana, had been in his father's family for three generations. His father was reluctant to leave; Castro would certainly fall. Efraín wrote her one last time before he turned eighteen.

Now, decades later, he remembers the veranda that wrapped around his house in Havana. He has hazy memories of Soledad, the maid who prepared his noonday lunches while his mother played Canasta with her manicured friends. And while he can no longer conjure his mother's face, he remembers her voice in her letter.

Understand, niño, we cannot leave what is ours.

When he turned eighteen the orphanage provided a one-way bus ticket to any place he wanted to go. He'd received letters from Rafaelito, frequently at first when he left to join his family in Florida, more sporadically as the years went on. Rafaelito wrote that he and his family lived in Tampa, much further north than Miami, but warm nevertheless. He told Efraín that Tampa had a boulevard called Bayshore which hugged the bay the way the Malecón did in Havana, and although waves didn't come crashing over the seawall as they did on the Malecón, it was still quite a sight to see.

Efraín now wondered if the address was missing a number or had an extra one. It couldn't be any further west. The avenue changed names shortly past the condo complex as it crossed a large intersection and became a curving tree-lined road leading into well-established neighborhoods.

He decided to turn around and head east.

Traffic moved slowly as they passed the mini-mart from where they'd started, continuing east, under the interstate over-pass. The area changed abruptly on the other side of the interstate. He drove through Suitcase City, a low-rent area of town where worn hookers, homeless people pushing shopping carts, and scab-skinned meth-heads roamed the streets.

Efraín drove on diligently on the lookout for an address he was now starting to believe didn't exist. The dimming winter sun cast a yellow shadow, and he felt his ankle begin to throb. He asked the woman about her family, making conversation to keep the pain in his foot at bay.

"Tengo cinco hijos," the woman said, telling Efraín of the five children she'd left in Mexico with her mother, and how she sent money every month to keep them fed. She'd followed the crops alone for almost two years, and now her brother was here. It would be easier, verdad, with someone?

"It must be so hard," Efraín said mindlessly, and the obviousness of his statement actually shamed him.

"I do whatever destiny asks," she said. She smoothed her gray sweatpants, and delicately placed her crossed palms on top of one knee. "Y usted, señor? What is your work?"

"Techos."

He'd come from Nebraska to the house of Rafaelito's parents where for a short time he was allowed to stay. Construction work was readily available, and even though he had no skills, he could hit a nail with a hammer. A friend of Rafaelito's family found him work framing roofs. Efraín swung himself across the trusses under a hot Florida sky, vengefully pounding nails. He peeled off his shirt and let the sun blister his skin. Sweat poured from his body. He finished each day with aching muscles, and a profound exhaustion that gratefully brought him sleep.

Two weeks after meeting Emelina behind the palmettos, he saw her again at a birthday party for one of Rafaelito's cousins. From a distance, he watched Emelina dance in the living room; then watched as she headed for the back door and followed her to the corner of the yard where rose bushes surrounded a thigh-high, plaster San Lázaro.

"Caught me again," she said.

"What?" he asked, "no cigarettes?"

Emelina giggled, "No cigarettes, but too much sidra. Do you dance?"

Efraín shook his head.

Before he realized what was happening, Emelina leaned his way and kissed him, softly and fully. At eighteen, he had never been kissed before.

"Seems there are two things I'm going to have to teach you," Emelina said.

Efraín stood there breathing hard, his face burning, and said nothing.

"I had a boyfriend," she motioned with her head, "back there. An official boyfriend. Comprometida. My father said we could get married when I turned twenty."

"What," Efraín started and cleared his throat, finding his voice, "happened?"

"He didn't want to come with us when we had the chance to leave," she said. "There was room in the boat, but I guess he loved the revolution more than me. He sent a picture a few months ago. He's standing by a truck, holding a large transistor radio. He wrote he'd won it cutting sugar cane—he was the first to meet the required quota. I sent him back a picture of *me* with a radio. I told him I'd won mine by eating ham." Emelina turned around quickly and went back into the house, leaving Efraín alone in the yard.

In her sing-song voice the woman recounted the names and ages of her children, adding some detail about each, telling him Roberto, her eldest, ate whole tomatoes the way americano children ate apples, and Luisita, her youngest, was afraid of thunder. Then she told him her husband was gone. Se nos fue, she said, and Efraín chose not to ask if she meant he'd died or had abandoned them. And when he said nothing, because he didn't know what to say, she asked if he was married.

"Sí," Efraín nodded, "sí, señora, sí."

In the same way Efraín found roofing work; knowing someone, or someone who knew someone, he found a small room to rent. Two years later as they both turned twenty, to his happy surprise, he married lovely Emelina.

One night in bed, while on their brief honeymoon, Emelina held her arm towards him, her wrist pulse side up. "Bite me," she said.

Efraín let out a snicker, shook his head puzzled, and pushed her arm away.

"Do it," she said. "Bite me!"

When he said no, Emelina grabbed his arm and sunk her teeth into his flesh. Efraín yelped and yanked his arm away.

Emelina looked directly into his eyes. "Remember this," she said. "You couldn't, but I could." She took his arm again and gently licked the red crescents her teeth had left, then she trailed her tongue up his arm, across his chest, and down his body.

"Y usted y su esposa?" the woman asked. "Do you have children?"

Efraín shook his head. They were stopped. The truck idled as they waited for traffic to move, but Efraín did not look her way.

"Qué lástima!" the woman said, and having expressed her pity, fell silent.

Emelina had lost six. The first one they conceived and lost before their first anniversary. Ten years later, the last one, the one she carried the longest, bled out of her before she'd reached the third trimester, even though she'd diligently stayed in bed for weeks.

"You can leave too," Emelina had said to him. "I don't need you to stay."

They continued along, leaving behind Suitcase City and entering the part of Fletcher Avenue that housed medical offices, and backed the research area of the university.

"It is not here, is it?" the woman asked.

It was time to turn around. Efraín looked at her, "Do you know anyone else?"

"No."

They drove in silence, through the early dusk, back the way they came. Efraín felt a weight deep within him, as he considered options. He could drive her to a shelter, rent her a motel room, take her home; what would Emelina say?

They were now reentering Suitcase City again, when she said loudly, "There. Stop there."

"Where?" He looked where she pointed.

In a strip shopping center, housed between an Amscot and a nail parlor, was a small storefront; the sign above it was a replica of the Mexican flag labeled Productos Mexicanos. The storefront window read: Tomatillos, Masa Harina, Envíos Directos.

"That's not the address," Efraín said.

"It does not matter."

Efraín parked in front. He grimaced as he stepped down from the truck and walked to the passenger side. He intended to help her with her bags, but she was already out of the truck, possessions in hand, holding tightly to what was hers.

"Señora, are you sure?" Efraín asked uncomfortably.

She nodded, reached in her pocket, and pulled a crumbled five-dollar bill. Before she could offer it to him, Efraín held up his hands, palms flat, firmly saying no, hoping it wouldn't be an insult if he offered her some money.

She draped her knapsack over her shoulder, touched his arm and said in her melodic Spanish, "God will pay you in his glory."

Efraín sat in the truck and watched her enter the market. The heat from the vents suddenly felt stifling and he turned it off, noticing that the floury corn scent lingered even though she'd gone.

Finally, with an oppressive sense of loss, he drove away.

When Efraín entered his house, it was filled with the pungent smell of sofrito. He closed the door quickly against the cold.

"Efraín!" Emelina said loudly. She walked towards him, wiping her hands on a dish towel. "You left your cell here."

Efraín opened his mouth to speak, but Emelina didn't give him a chance. "Where have you been?" she asked, and he saw genuine worry in her eyes. "You're gone forever, it's dark, and you're out there with that damn foot of yours, all descojona'o. You hear all the time about people having strokes, forgetting where they live."

Emelina reached out and took his hands in hers, "What happened, viejo, did you get lost?"

FOR IF THE FLIES

IN THE VINEGARY LIGHT OF THE bathroom mirror, my face reminds me of Tío Domingo. It's just the cheeks. As I've aged, mine have plumped and gotten fuller. My uncle's cheeks have always been full and round. Sometimes our resemblance surprises me. Not when I'm putting on makeup or fixing my hair, but when I glimpse myself unexpectedly in the windows of buildings, the mirrored walls of stores, or now, barely awake at five in the morning, in the unforgiving light of his bathroom.

I smell Cuban coffee.

I enter the kitchen, expecting to find him, but instead it's Tía Teresa at the counter in her faded lavender nightgown. I yawn and kiss the back of her head. "Buenos días, Tía. What are you doing?"

She turns toward me, a mayonnaise-smeared spatula in her hand. "Making sandwiches for your fishing trip."

"Tía," I start softly, "we fixed sandwiches last night, remember?" Yesterday, in preparation for the fishing trip, we bought Cuban bread, Serrano ham, and a wedge of red-waxed cheese at the bodega.

My aunt looks at me, blank and distant, and then suddenly, she is present.

"Ay, niña." Tía Teresa shakes her head at the sandwiches. She takes a deep breath that puffs out her chest and straightens her shoulders.

I take a deep breath too, to stop burgeoning tears.

"Bueno," Tía shrugs, "now you have more, por si las moscas."

Por si las moscas. I haven't heard that in a long time, and a small laugh escapes me. Literally translated, it's nonsensical: for if the flies. But idiomatically, it's a precautionary action. It's something you do just in case because, well, because you just never know. If the Boy Scouts were a Cuban organization, that should be their motto. Why be prepared when you could be "for if the flies?"

Tío Domingo joins us in the kitchen, "Mi niña, ready?"

Sliding fast down the other side of fifty, I'm still my aunt and uncle's niña.

"Un cafécito and I'm good to go," I say.

Tío Domingo notices the sandwiches, his eyes meet my aunt's, and she shakes her head.

"No importa, Teresa." He leans into her, kissing her cheek. "We can have those for lunch tomorrow." When Tío Domingo turns and I see his face, I realize that this, and not the fishing trip, is why my uncle was so insistent when he called two nights ago.

I hesitated before answering when his name displayed on the caller ID. Not because I didn't want to speak with him, but because feigning cheerfulness took too much effort. "Niña, come fishing this weekend," Tío had said when I picked up. "When was the last time we went fishing? When was the last time you even visited?"

"Ay, Tío, it's not a good time."

"Now is the perfect time, niña. The weather is good. No more summer rains, not too hot, not too cold. I told your father I want to go out one more time before we change the clocks."

"Because you think the fish bite better during Daylight Savings?"

"No, cabrona, because you know it takes me weeks to adjust, and then it will be too cold."

Born and raised in Cuba, my uncle has lived in Florida for close to fifty years. To him, cold is anything below sixty-eight degrees.

"I don't think I can get away," I said.

The company where I've worked for twenty-five years is downsizing, just another lingering casualty from The Great Recession. I'm one of the lucky ones. I still have a job. But I've seen what's happened to many of my coworkers. They're out there, résumé in hand, looking for work for the first time in years. It's frightening. I go to the office early and leave late. I telecommute on weekends trying to make myself indispensable.

"You have to make time," Tío said. "And stay with your aunt and me instead of your parents. They get to see you more often."

When I started to refuse again, Tío interrupted. "Elena, it's been too long since you've been home."

My uncle never calls me by my name.

I arrived by lunchtime yesterday.

"Nilda is coming over soon," Tío Domingo now says to my aunt, insisting he help put away the extra sandwiches before we leave. "She wants to keep you company. Remember? You're going shopping today."

"We're eating lunch at the mall."

Tío nods. "You're eating lunch at the mall."

Nilda is my mother. Tío Domingo is her younger brother. He was sixteen when I was born. When I was four years old and housebound with the chicken pox, he came over every day, and we set up camp on the couch. We played Siete y Media and Old Maid and had calamine-dipped cotton ball fights.

When he turned twenty-one he married Tía Teresa, and I sprinkled flowers at their wedding.

A few years later we were all refugees in the United States.

When I was ten, Tía Teresa gave birth to my cousin Dominguito after a difficult pregnancy and a harrowing delivery. There could be no more children for them. Tío Domingo said that was all right; he had me, his niña, and now he had his boy.

When I was twenty-eight I helped him bury Dominguito.

It was July, a month after my cousin's high school graduation.

The roads were wet from summer afternoon rain. He was on his way to meet friends, headed north on Gulfshore Boulevard where the road curves, and he fishtailed. Dominguito hit two oleander trees. He hit the first one sideways, then bounced off and hit the other. The second tree pinned him to the car, the first one fell on top of him. My uncle masked his grief by saying that not only had he lost his son and a car, but fuck if he didn't have to pay for two new oleander trees.

Tía Teresa's mind started to wander then. Suddenly she'd get a look on her face, and you knew she'd drifted away. It wasn't that she couldn't remember; it was that she couldn't forget.

It was hard for me to forget, too. I wasn't just Dominguito's cousin. I was the sibling he didn't have. I was his third parent, the one who cared for him after school and during summer vacations while my aunt and uncle worked. With my young cousin's death, I stopped being those things and became something else. I was still the daughter my aunt and uncle never had, but now I was the son they could no longer hug. The milestone events of my life were doubly celebrated: the promising promotion that transferred me to a different town; my marriage to Nick; the birth of our son, Dominic—named partially for his father and partially for the boy who didn't live. They weren't just my experiences; they were the ones Dominguito would never have. I sheltered Tío Domingo and Tía Teresa. I played up the happy for them and toned down the sad.

Which is why, as I struggle to keep my job, I've kept my distance for months.

Outside, the dampness of a humid night is visible in the dew that drips from Tío's truck. Faint pink light edges the morning sky and a hint of coolness blends with the still-present moisture signaling a turn in the seasons. There is nothing to pack except a large cooler. Tío keeps the fishing gear stored on his boat at the marina. The cooler is heavy with ice, drinks, sandwiches, and bagged squid for bait. I reach for one end to help lift it, but Tío Domingo shoos me away. Squaring his legs in a sumo wrestler's stance, he lifts the cooler onto the cargo hold and groans. "Coño, it's heavy."

The roads to the marina are completely empty at this early hour on a Saturday. Coquina Shores, where I grew up, where Tío and Tía and my parents live, is a solid four-hour drive, down the Florida peninsula and west to the Gulf. We cross streets whose names I've always known but seem vaguely unfamiliar as we drive the Tamiami Trail. The arteries of the town are the same, but the shops and buildings are different—what was once a local hardware store is now a sprawling Walmart.

"It's incredible how much the town has grown," I say. "Remember how it used to be when we first got here? Everything was new and it seemed so big. For the longest time, I didn't know it was tiny." When we came it was the mid-sixties, and the town was less than a quarter of the size it is today.

"You liked the automatic doors in all the grocery stores." My uncle grins. "You'd never seen them before."

Tío Domingo shakes his head. "I tell you, I drive this town every day and sometimes even I don't recognize it. And it confuses your aunt."

"Why didn't you tell me she'd gotten so bad?"

"You have your own troubles." He stares ahead at the empty road. "There are good days and bad ones. She can't drive anymore. She got lost coming home from Publix. Teresa doesn't remember how long she drove around before she pulled over and called me. You know where I found her? Way north of town by that new hotel. She was sitting in the car shivering like a wet dog when I found her."

"When was this?"

"Three days ago."

"Ay, Tío. Why didn't you tell me when you called?"

He shrugs. "I'm telling you now, niña. It's like your aunt enters a bubble of forgetfulness, then the bubble pops." Tío smacks his lips for emphasis. "And she's herself again. She remembers the names of neighbors back in Cuba she hasn't seen in decades, but she can't remember she made sandwiches last night. Listen to this, last week I bought mangos at la bodega and she tells me that Ignacia—you don't remember her, she lived down the street from us in Pinar del Río—Teresa tells me Ignacia was allergic to mangos. Actually," he pinches the air with his thumb and index finger, "not the mango itself, just the skin because it has a chemical similar to poison ivy and some people react to it. De veras, she tells me all this."

He sits up, gripping the steering wheel with both hands, his arms straight, "Next day, she forgot she had macaroni boiling on the stove and went out to work in the yard. She heard the smoke detector; that's the only reason she came back inside. Tú sabes, niña, that's the most difficult part. I mean, the past is the past, the good and the bad. It's the present. It's just really hard to live through the day when you can't remember the present. I try to be around as much as possible. Your mother comes over often. The family helps. Qué se le va a hacer? On a bad day, there are just too many bubbles."

I hear the resignation in his voice. He's been playing the sheltering game as well.

"Look," he says, "the old Dairy Queen is still the same." We head west toward the Gulf. In the glow of dawn, the road stretches long before us dotted with red, amber, and green traffic lights; a string of bright beacons guiding us toward the sea.

My father and Tío Samito are waiting at the marina. Papi grins at me. My father's face is long and lean. Although he didn't give me the leanness of his face, he did give me his olive eyes, the ones my grandmother gave him. We had dinner together last night in the home where I grew up: my parents, Tío Domingo, Tía Teresa, and me.

Tío Samito steps toward me. He's not my real uncle; he's my tío postizo, my artificial uncle, like dentures. He's Tía Teresa's brother, and I haven't seen him in a year. Heels together he gives me an old-world bow and kisses the top of my hand. "Let's take a look at you." He holds me at arm's length by the shoulders. Three times divorced, at seventy-four, Samito is short, stocky and boxer tough with raisin-like skin acquired from spending as much time as possible on his motorcycle. Yet he is graceful, with a natural charm that makes a kiss on the hand unaffected. He still runs a motorcycle shop. He can fix and restore them. The baby boomers' fascination with bikes provides Samito with so much business he says it'd be a sin to quit.

Once on the boat, I bring in the bumpers and sit on a rear seat as we pull away from the marina. The boat cuts through the tea-colored water slowly as we follow the channel markers, heeding the Make-No-Wake signs. Mangroves grow along the shoreline. Their spider-like legs arch toward the brackish water that turns lighter as we get closer to the pass where we'll leave the Intracoastal and enter the Gulf. I stand and turn around to see the land as we leave it behind. Tío Domingo looks over his shoulder; Papi and Samito look backwards as well. The men are quiet. They've left land behind before.

We enter the pass and my uncle shouts a hang-on warning, then he pushes the throttle and the speed lifts up the bow. I cup my hands around my mouth and shout to get his attention, and when he turns, I point to the front of the boat. He nods, giving me a thumbs-up. I maneuver to the front trying to keep my balance because Tío never lets down on the speed. I sit at the very tip and grab hold of the chrome railing. The boat rises with each swell and drops back to the water with a thud. My body moves forward with each rise and backward with each drop. Spray from the now clear, green water hits my skin, drying quickly in the wind, leaving behind traces of salt. I close my eyes and drop my head back. I love it. I'd forgotten how much I love it.

Tío Domingo slows the boat to trolling speed and monitors a small screen. It bleeps occasionally and he signals my father to look. There's much head nodding, and my uncle cuts the engine.

"Ready to catch fish?" he asks.

"How you fishing?" Papi asks me. "Rollo or rod?"

"Let's start with rollo for old time's sake. If I don't have any luck, I'll switch."

A rollo is just a spool of heavy test line. You cast it lasso-style above your head, and wear a small strip of rubber tubing on your index finger, guarding it from cuts, while the line dangles in the water. When a fish strikes, you pull like mad and someone with a net comes to help. That's the way they fished in Cuba. It's the way they taught me to fish.

I apply sunscreen before my hands start smelling like bait and strip to my bathing suit.

"You put on weight," Samito says.

I cringe because I know it.

"Looks good, like your mother," he adds. "That Nilda, she gets better with age."

"It's the great sex that keeps her mother young," Papi teases.

"Sí?" Tío Domingo laughs. "Who's she sleeping with?"

"Hey, I have my little blue pill."

"Coño, chico," Samito grins. "I get those so regularly I asked my tax guy if I could claim my pharmacist as a dependent."

When I laugh, Samito asks, "Haven't you missed your old men hablando mierda?"

"I think I've missed a lot of things. Tía is . . ."

"Tía is shopping with your mother today, and we are fishing," Tío Domingo says and hands me a spool.

I see Tío Samito shake his head. My father cuts up squid. Tío Domingo gives me a chunk, I bait my hook and cast. Samito and Papi follow. Tío Domingo casts last.

The day has lifted. Free of clouds, the sky is now an endless blue. The Gulf is calm and the boat sways on the water. Forty minutes later, Papi has caught one yellow snapper, and that's it. Tío Domingo suggests we try another spot, but Samito wants to stay. He says we need to make an offering to Yemayá for luck, and takes five beers from the cooler, pouring one into the sea.

There is Gatorade among the beers, which I'd prefer this early on an empty stomach, but I refuse to be the wimp in a group of old men. "Take out sandwiches too, Samito. The fish aren't the only ones who need to eat."

The first time I went fishing with my father and uncles—not off the pier or sitting by some canal but real fishing, miles out in the Gulf—I was nineteen and Dominguito was alive. Before that, I'd never been allowed to go. Tío Domingo and Papi bought a boat several years after we'd been in the States. Not like this one, much smaller. Other relatives and friends had similar boats as well. Fifteen-foot bow riders perfect for the Intracoastal or following the shore, sturdy crafts that sped toward open water. There is safety in numbers there. They went out together as a small fleet.

The men worked routinely from sunrise to sunset. They left for work every morning to paint houses, hang drywall, put down sod, do yard maintenance; dirty, plentiful work in the booming state of Florida. They spent their days in grimy clothes that looked filthy even when they came out of the wash, and they donned them dutifully as they worked haggardly from day to day. But on fishing days they came alive. Bare-chested, wearing shorts free of work dirt, they set off before the sun rose, coolers packed with bait and beer. They returned reeking of fish, sunburned and tipsy conquerors gloriously bearing their catch.

On those evenings we'd gather at someone's house for a fish fry.

The women cooked the fish. They never went on the trips. I was dying to go; I asked every time. It wasn't appropriate. It was a man thing. They got raunchy. I'd get seasick. There was no place for me to go to the bathroom. But then Tío Domingo and my father decided to take Dominguito out for the first time. "If he can go fishing," I demanded, "I can go. Who helps him with school assignments because I know English better than all of you? Who takes him to and from baseball practice?" I asked my uncle and my father. "I'm going fishing, too."

I had beer and sandwiches for breakfast. I jumped in the open water to pee and hid my fear by voicing the *Jaws* dah-dum sound. Maybe it was beginner's luck, maybe Yemayá decided to nudge the door open for me. Not two minutes after I'd swung the test line, dripping bait juice as it twirled above my head, I got a strike. The fish fought hard, and I gave up trying to wind the line around the spool, pulling hand over hand, ignoring offers of help and my bleeding palms. Fourteen pounds, and not just any fish, a grouper, *the* eating fish. There's a picture of me: a wadded mess of line at my feet, proudly holding the fish, its mouth open and body arced in a taxidermist's dream pose.

Papi and Samito are on opposite sides of the bow, lines dangling from one hand, sandwiches in the other, beer cans carefully placed between their knees. Tío Domingo and I are at the stern, side by side, talking softly.

"So," Tío says, wadding up his sandwich wrapper. "Your work? Explain to me, eh." He drains his beer, crushes the can, and gets another.

"The company is trying not to go under. Jobs got cut. We're expected to do more with less, but for now, at least I still have a job."

Tío points his chin at my beer and I finish it. He hands me another.

"A lot of people, they have to start over," he says.

I nod and sip my beer.

"It's hard starting over."

"When you came here, you didn't even have the language. People do what they have to do. But Tío, they don't have to do it alone."

"Domingo," Papi calls suddenly. "Aquí no pica nada, chico. You ready to try another spot? We need to move on."

My uncle looks at my father, looks at me, then goes and starts the boat.

We are out so far that all there is to see is water. To the west is the horizon, and to the east the coast is no longer visible. The boat bounces forward rhythmically. I sit on one of the middle seats and drop my head back, feeling the sun and wind on my face. Even with sunglasses, I can see the sun's orange glow behind my eyelids. The food, the beer, and the droning sound of the engine lull me into sleep until the men's shouts bolt me up. It's a pod of dolphins, their gray skin glistening as they arch in and out of the water. My father is grinning, and my uncles, too. They seem younger.

We stop to try our luck again. Tío Domingo wants a rod and reel, and he reaches past me where they're grouped in holders. When a swell rocks us, he grabs my shoulder to keep his balance and I reach out to steady him. He's wearing sandals secured by Velcro straps, and his feet, usually clad in sneakers, are pale. They seem vulnerable, and I look away.

We end up in the same positions on the boat. Samito quickly catches a grunt, and then another. I bring up a yellow snapper. Tío Domingo gets a grouper, but it's below regulation size and he drops it back. He sips his beer slowly before re-baiting his hook.

Time passes, no one has gotten another strike, and my uncle says to me, "On really bad days, your aunt gets agitated, so I bring her out here. Not this far out, I just hug the coast. We cruise slowly, and it soothes her. She likes it when I stop the engine and let the currents take us. Sometimes, she doesn't want to head back in, sometimes I'm the one that doesn't want to return, so we drift until we're both ready."

I look at him and listen.

"Sometimes, I don't want to return at all. I never expected it. It never occurred to me her mind would go like this," he says. "Y tan rápido, it's going so quickly. And there is nothing I can do. Nothing, except watch it happen."

"This isn't what you envisioned."

"What?" My uncle waves his arm around. "Look at this boat. Twenty-five-foot cuddy cabin—three-hundred-fifty cubic inch inboard. This is exactly what I envisioned." He rubs his hand across his face. "I just thought my son would be on it."

"I think about him," I say. "And you know, it's the silly things I remember, like when I'd pick him up from baseball practice all dirty and damp, smelling of onion sweat, and he'd tease threatening to hug me."

"Oye," Papi calls to us. "You two have been psst, pssting, like two gossiping old viejas most of the morning. If there's a good chisme, I want to know, too."

"Now who's an old gossip?" I ask.

"I'm ready for another sandwich," Samito says. "My fishing line is limp."

"Just like the rest of us," Papi says, "it just needs a little Vee-ag-ra."

Samito takes out a CD player. "What we need is music. We're not frightening anything away."

Celia Cruz sings about how she keeps life spicy. Samito makes his way to the beer cooler, singing along. He dances a couple of tight steps in place, gets his beer, looks our way, and brags, "I've still got it!"

"And I do *not* want to see any of it," Papi says.

"You've always been jealous of my moves."

"Are you still doing your tricky little disco-bembé-drop-the-handkerchief move?" I ask Samito.

"Can Celia sing?"

"Celia's dead."

"Coño, verdad que sí." Samito laughs. "It's hard to keep track these days. I drop my handkerchief every now and again, but I don't fall to a push-up to pick it up with my teeth anymore. Now I bend down, and pick it up with my hand," he wiggles his eyebrows, "with sex appeal."

"Sí," Tío Domingo laughs. "Last month he sex-appealed himself straight to the chiropractor."

Samito waves his hand dismissing him. He sits on the cooler and rubs a cold beer can on his forehead. "Tengo suerte. Seventy-four and two of my favorite things are still popular: motorcycles and Latin dancing. If I drop and don't get up, I die happy."

It's eleven o'clock, and even though it's early October, the sun is hot. We decide to try one last place, and if the fish still don't cooperate, we'll head back.

This time the four of us reach for rods. The spools are an old tradition, simple and uncomplicated, a throwback to places and times no one wants to forget, but they're not as functional. We hold the same positions we've had on the boat all day. Celia's music is no longer on, and we're quiet. The water is still. The whizzing of lines as they leave our reels cuts the silence, followed by hollow plops.

Tío Domingo is still next to me.

"We have to make arrangements," I say to him. "To help you help her. You can't take care of her by yourself."

"The family helps," Tío says. "Nilda. Your father. Ask Samito." Tío calls out, "Right Samito? Everybody helps with Teresa?"

"You know we can't leave her alone anymore, Domingo," Samito says. "She has to be watched por si las moscas. What if instead of boiling pasta she'd decided to fry something the other day?"

"Even with the family's help, Tío, it's too much. You know it is."

Tío Domingo's shoulders go slack, he reels his line in slowly and he shakes his head. "I can't put her away, as if she were nothing, send her away."

I feel the pressure of tears rising, prickling my scalp and overwhelming my eyes, and I blink them back. "It doesn't have to be like that. There are agencies, there are people, people trained to help and . . ." My uncle's eyes look as lost and distant as Tía Teresa's did this morning. "Tío, I can make the calls. I know how to get information. I'll help you figure it out, okay?"

Tío nods at me, blinking tightly.

"Ay, coño. Now what?" Samito asks.

I think he's talking to us, but he's talking to his reel. Somehow Samito's line has gotten tangled with my father's. Tío Domingo gingerly makes his way to the front of the boat to help. I reel in as well. I watch them together, talking over each other and at the same time, six hands on the knots. I know that's how I'll remember their hands.

I'm thankful for sunglasses, because this time I can't stop my tears. I wipe them away and breathe deeply. I stand at the stern, take off my sunglasses and look at the water. No matter what comes next, today is a good day. Raising my arms, I arch my body, and dive into the sea, swimming down, rushing. I swim until my lungs can't take any more and flip up. I focus on the sunlight above, and scissor-kick, breaking through the surface. When I dog-shake the salt water off my face, I see them peering down at me.

"Pero, estás loca?" my father asks of me. "What are you doing? Mira eso, Domingo. And no life jacket on her!"

"Niña, did you have to make pipi? This boat has a head, you know," Tío Domingo says.

"This is more fun," I say. And dah-dumming loudly, I backstroke a circle around the boat.

They cheer me on with "dale, dale," shouts as I swim around the boat which drifts ever so slightly away with the flow of the current. When I've come full circle, I use the motor as a step, and they help me back in the boat.

With lines untangled and fresh beers opened, we fish. The muffled thumps of water lapping at the bottom of the boat keep a comfortable rhythm. It goes on for a long time; I don't really know for how long, until Samito sings, "Coño!"

Something is giving him a good fight.

"Aquí también," Papi says quickly, "aquí también."

His fishing pole bends toward the water. Papi leans forward as the fish takes out line, leans backward as he reels it in. Samito brings up his fish first. It dangles from his hook, but Tío Domingo is ready with the net and scoops it up: a fair size grouper. A keeper. Papi brings his in too, and Tío Domingo moves quickly from Samito to my father, net at the ready.

"Dinner!" Papi grins at his fish, another grouper, slightly larger than Samito's.

Although we stay a good while longer, each man recounting the story of his recent catch as if we hadn't all been there as witnesses, there are no more strikes. We begin to head back as the sun drops down the other side of noon. The return trip is slower. There is no hurry.

We'll gather to eat fish tonight at my uncle's house.

We see dolphins again. They swim in and out of the water, and we watch them until they stop surfacing. Then we follow their shadows until we lose them in the light shimmering off the sea.

EMELINA

EMELINA CHEWED A BITE OF PEAR and swallowed. She rubbed her thumb over the tips of her tingling fingers. Eating fruit supposedly helped with nicotine cravings, but so far, it hadn't. She could cheat and no one would know; the parking lot was empty. But she didn't have cigarettes. The four she allowed herself a day waited at home along with her husband. Emelina bit the pear again, chewing slowly, counting to ten. Nothing. She tossed the half-eaten fruit in the trash and headed for her car.

The drive from St. Anthony's Elementary School to her house took only fifteen minutes. October made the days shorter. By the time she pulled into her driveway, the late-afternoon amber light accented the pumpkins by her front door. Autumn is subtle in Tampa. The oppressive summer humidity lifted, the cypresses began to lose their needles, and green lawns turned sleepy brown. Emelina always felt a melancholy accompanied the season.

"Late day, Eme?" her husband, Efraín, called from his bedroom office when she entered the kitchen from the garage.

"Taking inventory of art supplies for the Christmas projects."

"Helping the kindergarteners make presents for their parents?" Efraín came to the kitchen. His sixty-eight-year-old body, still slim and tanned from years of working outdoors, leaned slightly to the right, taking pressure off his weak ankle.

"Same as we do every year, Efraín."

"Mail's on the counter."

Same as it is every day, Emelina stifled the urge to say. She took the cigarettes from the kitchen junk drawer, lit one quickly, and inhaled.

"Not changing clothes today?" he asked.

Emelina slowly blew out smoke, saying nothing.

"You shouldn't smoke inside the house," he said and walked away.

Emelina inhaled again. She stepped out of her shoes, flicked ashes in the sink, and tipped her head back, exhaling a prayer for patience.

Since the moment George, Efraín's longtime assistant, called sputtering through the news that her husband had fallen while inspecting a roof his company had finished, Emelina's time at home had stopped being her own. She used to come home to an empty house, leaving behind the noise of children and school bells. She had two, sometimes three hours, before Efraín arrived. The solitude centered her as she did house chores, gardened, cooked dinner. Her routine shattered two months back along with Efraín's ankle.

She'd nursed her husband for weeks after the surgery to pin his ankle back together. She fetched what he needed, aided him to and from the bathroom, helped him settle in the shower stool she purchased so he could bathe. Her husband stoically bore his pain. Not once did he complain, and that's what irritated her most. For days Efraín's eyes had that look of his, the one that reminded her of a neglected dog, starving for a caress and terrified of it at the same time. Decades ago, that look had intrigued her. Early in their marriage, she'd tried to change it. When it remained constant, the intrigue came from seeing if she could make it worse until, that too, became tiresome.

Emelina squashed her cigarette butt into an ashtray and felt the tingling in her fingertips dissipate. She was down to four a day. This was the best she'd ever done. Nothing had worked before. The patch made her jittery and nicotine gum made her feel like a cow masticating cud. She was cutting back one cigarette a day every thirty days. At this rate, she'd quit completely in three months. She'd learned long ago that giving up just a little at a time was tolerable.

Emelina leaned against the kitchen counter and flipped through the mail, tossing junk to one side and bills to the other. At the bottom of the stack, to her delight, was the Las Palmeras news magazine. This issue was thick, almost twenty pages.

She walked barefoot to the living area that opened from the

kitchen, news magazine in one hand, cigarette in the other, and settled on the couch. She propped her feet on the coffee table and clicked the remote. She didn't really want to watch television, but she'd found that if she pretended to watch, Efraín didn't make conversation and left her alone.

Emelina opened the cover page, which was always the same: *Las Palmeras en el Exilio* below a waving Cuban flag.

The first few pages had grainy black and white photos of some function or place in Las Palmeras, taken in Cuba either before or in the first years following the revolution. She studied each picture looking for a face she might know, her long-dead parents, maybe a relative, or a friend. In one picture, taken at a ladies' luncheon circa 1956, a stout, elegantly dressed woman pinned a corsage on someone she did recognize: her friend Elisa's mother.

The next page had the usual tiresome poem beseeching the Cuban populace to stay strong in the face of ever-lasting tyranny, this one written by a butcher from Hialeah. A woman from New Jersey wrote about the gardens of the Parque Central in Las Palmeras, the park of her youth, to this day the loveliest she'd ever seen. The magazine's center had a reminder for the annual town reunion. Always held in early November, and always held in Miami. She and Efraín attended every year. This year, because of his accident, she'd forgotten to buy tickets, but there was still time.

Emelina skimmed the list of people already committed

to attend. All the regulars were there: her cousin César and his family, Elisa and her husband, Elisa's brother and his wife, and then Emelina stopped short. Basilio Campos. She stared at the name for a moment; it couldn't have been more than a moment, but her cigarette burned to a finger of ash that dropped on her pants. "Coño." She brushed the ashes off, and the magazine fell to the floor.

"Eme?" Efraín emerged from the bedroom office at the end of the short hallway that separated the three bedrooms from the living area.

"What?"

"Qué te pasa?"

"Nothing's wrong," Emelina rose and returned to the kitchen. "Chicken for dinner," she said, her back to Efraín, her hands toward the refrigerator.

After dinner, Efraín retreated to his office. Emelina turned on the dishwasher. She opened the junk drawer and took out her last two cigarettes of the day, picked up the magazine from the floor, and headed outside. The night sky was clear, and a thin breeze made the evening comfortable. Emelina breathed in the night air. With the summer rains over, the air had a crispness that promised cooler days. She sat on a patio chair in the almond semi-circle of a flood light and lit a cigarette, keeping the magazine closed on her lap. No need to open it, she knew the name was there.

The first time she saw Basilio, she'd smoked her first cigarette. It was at a party at Elisa's house and a breeze blew that evening as well. It was March and Emelina was seventeen, hot from dancing in a group of women: friends, mothers, aunts, each taking individual turns in the circle's center undulating to the drum beats. She'd walked outside to cool off. She bounced down the veranda stairs to the backyard seeking the breeze, and when she found it, she faced it, head back, eyes closed, her arms spread like wings. The wind dried the dampness of her skin.

"You dance with the music in your blood."

When Emelina turned around, tea-brown eyes smiled at her. She can never recall, certainly not for lack of trying, what she said, or if she said anything at all. He took two cigarettes from a pack in the breast pocket of his guayabera, lit them at the same time, and handed one to her—not asking if she wanted one or even if she smoked. She took the cigarette between her fingers, holding it the way she'd seen actresses do in movies.

He was Elisa's brother's new friend. Basilio asked her to dance, and under the watchful eyes of her mother, he glided her through the whispers.

Arturo's friend; just moved to Las Palmeras; he comes from Cienfuegos; his father has something to do with the government.

Emelina couldn't remember the music, and she couldn't quite remember the dance. She remembered that Basilio, slightly taller than she, laced his fingers snugly through her hand, and kept his other hand firmly at the curve of her back, sending currents through her.

Sergio, her father, was not pleased; his daughter with a Communist. But her father—the well-mannered pharmacist who prided himself on his refinement who, a year later, would clean toilets at a hospital in a country where he couldn't understand the language—graciously welcomed Basilio into his living room the first time he came to call.

"No te embulles," he told her once Basilio's visit was over. "This will not go forward."

Emelina knew it would regardless of what her father said. She'd felt the same currents from Basilio even though he sat respectfully a room's length away. She felt him the way she felt the beat of the music when she danced. He was in her blood.

Over the next two weeks, they met secretly three times. Basilio spoke fervently of his belief in the revolution and the Cuba the Comandante was creating. Emelina didn't really have an opinion nor cared one way or another about any of it, but she was mesmerized by the passion in Basilio's voice and the enthusiasm on his face as he spoke.

She was willful, but she wasn't stupid. The town was small. Almost everybody in Las Palmeras knew everybody else. When her father, who usually capitulated to her whims—the privilege of being an only child—again prohibited her from seeing Basilio, who was not only a Communist, but the son of a rising member of the Party, Emelina said something she'd always regret.

"I can't see Basilio because you don't agree with his politics. You know, his father might just be interested in that."

She'd said it with a checkmate attitude, triumphantly. But the stunning fluctuation of her father's face—shock, disappointment, deep hurt, and fear—made Emelina want the words back instantly.

"I didn't mean that," she took a step toward him, and he took a step back. "I didn't mean that, Papi. I would never do such a thing."

He put his hand up as if stopping traffic. "This world, Emelina, is unfair and unpredictable, even treacherous. I can't teach you that. You have my permission to see this young man, not because I'm afraid of you, but because I'm afraid for you. There are things you have to learn for yourself."

She started to speak, but her father kept his stop hand up.

"These courtships, they usually lead to marriage. I only ask you to wait on such a commitment until you're twenty. Yes?"

Humbled, ashamed, Emelina nodded her bowed head and her father turned and walked away.

The classroom lights were turned off for naptime. Emelina sat at her desk placing stickers on letter drawings by the light of the window. Dios, how many times had she counted to ten today itching for a cigarette, and every time she counted, Basilio Campos came to mind. She'd trained her memories of Basilio not to come unbidden. It had required dedicated discipline. The first year had been the hardest.

Her parents hadn't planned to leave Cuba. It happened. It was October then, too. 1965.

She and Basilio had been courting for seven months. Weeknights, he'd visit after dinner as customary. Most nights, in the company of her mother, they walked down to the Parque Central. There, she and Basilio branched off and visited with friends while her mother visited with equally vigilant mothers or maiden aunts assigned chaperoning duties. When they remained at home, Emelina noticed, if Basilio's conversation turned to politics, her father excused himself claiming tasks that required his attention.

In late September, Fidel Castro opened the port of Camarioca allowing Cubans to leave by boat if relatives from the United States came for them. A telegram arrived a week later. Her uncle, her mother's brother, was coming to get them.

"We're leaving," her father told her. "And it will break our hearts if you don't come with us. It's important to listen to your heart, but mija, it's foolish not to use your brain."

Emelina had listened to Basilio's conversations. She'd started paying attention. She compared his beliefs of everybody working equally for the common good to the reality of the hardships people were facing—empty stores, rations cards for products, lines for blocks when toothpaste or shoes arrived at stores. And worse still, the injustice of not being able to freely express contradictory opinions without fear. She also listened to her parents' quiet conversations. A fellow pharmacist, one town over, had been arrested for counter-revolutionary activities. There was no trial; he'd disappeared. Their longtime neighbor was arrested for buying a butchered hog on the black market. He'd been turned in by the area's head of the Comité, the vigilance committee. The neighbor was sent to jail, but the Comité leader, for performing her duties so well, was permitted to keep some of the meat.

The Camarioca Boatlift happened quickly. Within two days of her uncle's telegram, her parents were packing to leave. On the mid-October morning when they left Las Palmeras for the port of Camarioca, Emelina stood outside her house and watched a government official paste a seal on the door. Their home wasn't theirs anymore; it belonged to the government. One last time, Basilio asked Emelina not to leave. And one last time she begged him to go with her. After a sad and angry kiss, she clung to him wishing she could soak him into her pores.

After arriving home from work the following afternoon, Emelina opened the refrigerator contemplating dinner options. "What's this?" she asked her husband. There was a new carton of eggs, margarine, a bag of salad, and fresh deli ham.

"I made a trip to Publix for a few things today," Efraín said.

"And the ankle?"

"Not bad. I'm going back to work next week. You know, not all day, just checking things out. Give George a hand. Get out of your hair a little."

Emelina took a cigarette from the pack in the junk drawer but didn't light it. "I'll smoke it outside."

"Eme? I saw the Las Palmeras magazine. The party is coming up."

"Same as it does every year, Efraín."

"And?"

If he'd seen the magazine, he'd seen the list. She'd told Efraín about Basilio during one of their first conversations. She hadn't kept him a secret. What she kept from Efraín were the many times, early in their relationship, when with her closed eyes, his caresses became Basilio's. She knew what he was asking. "I don't know, Efraín."

Outside, Emelina lit a cigarette, and turned on the garden hose, lightly spraying her small fall garden of potted cherry tomatoes, basil, and leaf lettuce.

The first year she'd spent in Tampa, she'd ached for Basilio and hated him at the same time. She longed for his warm breath by her ear, the roughness of his tongue on hers, to feel how he grew stiff rubbing against her, and the wetness that oozed out of her when they were able to steal brief, unsupervised moments. Stupid. Stupid Basilio for not choosing her; for not choosing here. If he could have seen. If he could have seen the stores of Tampa. The shelves full of meat and soap. Air-conditioned cinemas. Clean streets devoid of soldiers.

When she couldn't keep desire and anger separate, she became agitated, wanting to turn her skin inside out. Cigarettes calmed her, and then all that she felt was lonely.

She'd recognized that loneliness in Efraín.

She met him one afternoon in 1966, at a get-together given by friends of her father. Efraín was a Pedro Pan boy. His parents had sent him unaccompanied to the United States in 1962 fearing for his future under the new regime. Like so many Pedro Pan kids, he'd thought the separation would be temporary, but years passed and his parents never came. His mother refused to leave Cuba, steadfastly believing Castro would fall. He and Emelina had that in common. They'd left, and the person with the tightest hold of their heart wouldn't follow.

Efraín was tall; he was muscular and tanned from time spent in the sun hammering roofs. He was shy, spoke softly, and at gatherings often sat to the side. Emelina was the aggressor. When she saw him at a party a few weeks later, she asked him to dance. She took what she'd learned from Basilio and used it with Efraín. Startling him with an unexpected first kiss, pressing against him the way

Basilio had pressed into her. But always, even after they married, she made sure in subtle ways that he knew she loved him less than he loved her.

Efraín never demanded more.

Then, before their first year of marriage was over, there was the baby that left before she could give him life, taking a piece of Emelina's heart with him. And so did the next, and the next, and the next. They were boys, even when it had been too early to tell, she knew they had been boys. Girls would have held on. Emelina believed it was blood—the way it passed from mother to daughter. The blood a woman shed was her mother's blood. Daughters wouldn't have left her body before it was time. By the time Emelina had her sixth and last miscarriage, she was thirty-one.

Emelina was coiling the garden hose into place when Efraín came to join her. He balanced on his cane.

"Tomatoes are coming in well," he said and took a step closer.

"Careful, ground is wet."

She sat in her usual garden chair, by the corner of the lanai, and Efraín sat next to her.

"The Palmeras party, Eme? You should go."

Emelina looked at the yard and not at Efraín, "What about your ankle? I can drive, but more than four hours in the car?"

"I'm not going. But you should go."

Emelina turned to look at him.

"Knowing that the sky above me could never be as blue as the sky of Cuba, Eme? That got old decades ago."

Parked outside the reunion hotel, Emelina lowered the windows in her car, turned the air conditioner fan to its highest setting, and twisted the vents to blow her way. She cupped her hand around a cigarette and lit it, breathing in and exhaling out the open window. When approached, she wanted to smell of Chanel No. 5, not nicotine. She'd arrived at the reunion an hour late on purpose. She didn't want to be there before Basilio. She wanted her entrance.

In past years, she and Efraín always came with Elisa and her husband. It'd become a tradition. The reunion had been held at the same Marriott ballroom for the past fifteen years. She and Efraín took Friday off to drive from Tampa to Miami. Although Elisa always offered her guest bedroom, Efraín insisted on a hotel room. He disliked staying in other people's homes because it reminded him of his Pedro Pan days when charity was his only option. The couples ate Friday night dinner out together. On Saturday, they met at Elisa's home for daiquiris—just like her mother made back home—Elisa said every year, raising her glass for the same toast, her wish and prayer: to a free Cuba, salud.

This year Emelina skipped all of it claiming she was tired from the long drive by herself, and in need of some solitude. "Ay, mija," she'd said to Elisa, "since his ankle, tú sabes, you know how it is, I don't get a moment to myself." Emelina didn't want to pretend that she didn't want—what? What did she want? To show Basilio she'd survived his abandonment. That she'd thrived in spite of it. To make him believe she'd never given him a second thought. To sashay her curves past him, for she still had her curves, and make him regret every moment since he chose not to get in the boat. She wanted all that and more.

Emelina flicked the cigarette butt out the open window and looked at her nails. Perfect. She'd had her nails and hair freshly done. She rubbed scented hand sanitizer through her fingers and checked her makeup in the rearview mirror. Outside the car, she adjusted the full-body Spanx beneath her ivy green dress—a green dark enough to slenderize, rich enough to accent her hazel eyes, and bold enough to stand out from the sea of black cocktail dresses.

The DJ played an old 1960s danzón by La Orquesta Aragón that Emelina recognized. She'd always loved the trilling sounds of the Aragón's flute, like a bird seductively calling for a mate. Instinctively, her shoulders gave a slight shimmy. She stood just outside the ballroom entrance, where she could see but not be seen, and scanned the room. Every year there were more unknown faces as new arrivals, people that came from Las Palmeras, but not the one she'd left behind decades ago, made their way to the States, and to the annual gathering.

Emelina stepped inside looking around the room and not

where she was walking. Someone bumped into her from the side and she turned.

"Look who's here! We thought you'd gotten lost." Elisa's husband kissed her cheek and said. "Come, come, your friend is right over here."

He took her elbow, guiding her through clusters of people talking, laughing, and congregating around circular tables. Some waved at her, others greeted her with loud, "Hola, chica," above the music which had shifted from the Aragón's danzón to Gloria Estefan's thumping—a warning or a threat—that the rhythm was going to get her. The nervous anticipation of the day, and the shift from her solitary thoughts to the raucous festivities, made Emelina dizzy.

"Eme!" Elisa jumped up to hug her. "Where have you been? Something wrong? I was worried."

"Just running a little late."

"I'll get you a drink," Elisa's husband said.

"Bueno, you look magnificent. That color, corazón, it's beautiful."

Emelina felt hands squeeze her shoulders from behind, at the same time Elsa said, "Look who's here!"

Emelina turned quickly. It was her cousin, César.

"Mi prima!" César, balder than the last time she'd seen him, kissed her cheek. His wife gave her a swift peck and they sat on either side of her at the table. "And, Efraín? Qué calamidad! How is his ankle?"

Before Emelina could respond, César began telling about his gallbladder; how it had to come out before another attack, because the last one was brutal, and his wife said that was nothing compared to her diverticulitis, and they asked about her cholesterol, but before she answered, they began expounding the healing properties of apple cider vinegar. Emelina swiveled her head between them.

Elisa's husband placed a drink in front of her and said, "Not me. Yo estoy entero." He pounded his chest. While the cousins asked him if he'd had a colonoscopy, Mariana, a secondary school friend from Las Palmeras, walked up. "Buenas, mi gente!" She blew Emelina a kiss across the expanse of the table and said something to Elisa that Emelina couldn't hear with the medical talk volleying around her, and the music blaring throughout the hall.

Emelina sipped her drink. The tips of her fingers tingled. The dance song came to an end, and the DJ said he was taking a break, declaring the buffet open.

Emelina heard Mariana say, "He's not here? Pity, but that's how those things go."

"Who?" Emelina heard the anxiousness in her voice, and she asked casually, "Who isn't here?"

"My brother," Elisa said. "Poor Arturo has the stomach flu."

César's wife began describing the one she'd suffered the previous month. Emelina excused herself saying she needed to find the restroom. What she needed was a cigarette. What if like Arturo,

Basilio wasn't here either? No one had mentioned him. Emelina walked through the lobby to the pool area. She could smoke out there. God, she missed the days when no one knew smoking was bad, when it was still elegant and sophisticated. Now she felt like a criminal, skulking, looking for a designated area with one of those hideous plastic long-necked tubs, the new millennium's sorry excuse for an ashtray.

It was pleasantly cool outside. Unlike Tampa, Miami had a breeze coming off the Atlantic. Emelina was glad to be away from the noise and the nonsense of her cousins. The pool had a bar and she sat on one of the stools. She made eye contact with the bartender, wiggling her unlit cigarette, and he nodded. Emelina pulled out a lighter and the young Latino, who had a stylish, short mohawk that reminded her of a kewpie doll, brought over a plastic ashtray, asking what she'd like.

"Rum and Coke." Emelina picked a speck of tobacco off the tip of her tongue.

"Cuba Libre, coming right up."

"Good," Emelina said to his back. "We've only been waiting more than fifty years."

"Do you think, perhaps, I may have one of your cigarettes? I'm all out," a gravelly-voiced man asked in Spanish, and sat on the next bar stool.

Emelina nodded and reached for her cigarette pack, when the

bartender brought her drink, asking if she wanted to pay or run a tab. She slid the pack the man's way. "Pay. I need to get back inside."

"Shame. Feel that breeze. Lighter?"

Emelina flicked her lighter and turned to face the man. He was thin with a yellow tinge. His face looked like a cashew—long, slim, and lightly curved in the middle—with the puckered muscles of someone who's lost their real teeth.

"Gracias, Eme. How are you, old friend?"

Emelina looked directly at the cashew man and saw tea-colored eyes. She felt her stomach sink and her body clench as if she were in a car that suddenly took a curve too fast.

"Basilio," she whispered.

"You look good, Eme."

Emelina took several fast drags, unsuccessfully trying to keep the fingers that held her cigarette from shaking, and looked Basilio up and down. She would've walked past this man inside, in the parking lot, on the street and not recognized him. A soft sadness rose up from her, stinging her eyes, but Emelina straightened and said firmly, "You don't."

When Basilio flinched, Emelina felt her fingers steady.

"Ha llovido mucho, Emelina. The years have been long."

"What are you doing here?"

"Same as you. The reunion."

"No, Basilio. What are you doing here?" Emelina circled her

arms. "How's that Cuba El Comandante created for you?"

"This life, Eme," Basilio pursed his lips. "Things don't always turn out the way you imagine. I arrived in January. Five years ago, my granddaughter married a Yuma she met en la Habana. He brought her over, and then she brought me. They live in West Palm Beach."

"And your wife?" Emelina didn't know if there had ever been a wife.

"She died nine, ten years ago. A childhood friend from Cienfuegos. She was a good woman. Y tú? Did you marry a good man?"

"I married a good boy who grew up to be a good man."

"Niños?"

"Things," Emelina tilted her chin and blew smoke his way, "don't always turn out the way you imagine."

"Eme, you and I ..."

"You and I made our choices, Basilio. We live with that." Emelina took a long drink from her glass and stood up. "Keep the cigarettes. I'm giving them up."

Emelina entered the lobby intending to return to the ballroom. Her legs were weak, and her hands, holding on to her purse, trembled. She felt disoriented. She sat in a plushy, oversized chair, and pressed her knees down to stop the shaking. The vibrant Basilio of her youth was gone, and the deteriorated man outside was someone she didn't recognize. What had she expected? Emelina texted Elisa, lying that maybe like poor Arturo, she too, had a stomach virus. She was leaving. Emelina could hear the DJ pumping up the crowd, challenging them to dance to one of their own, screaming, Pitbull! Emelina walked to the hotel doors, ignoring Elisa's offers of help, as the sounds of a song she didn't know faded away.

"Eme?" Efraín called from his bedroom office when she entered the house. "Is that you?" They met in the kitchen. "You're early. We never make it back until late afternoon."

"I left first thing this morning."

"But you didn't call?"

"Surprise." Emelina shrugged. She took a beer from the fridge. "Want one?"

"Why not, it's Sunday."

Emelina handed him a beer, opened the junk drawer, took out her cigarettes, and lit one. She waited for Efraín to object, but he didn't. "I'm down to three."

"That's the best you've done."

"It's the best I've done. Aren't you going to ask?"

"What do you want to tell me, Eme?"

"Do you always have to be so passive?"

"I am the way I am." Efraín took a sip of beer.

And he was. Efraín was nothing if not constant.

"Did you see your Basilio?"

"He stopped being my Basilio a long time ago. But, no, my Basilio wasn't there."

"And the party?"

"Same as it is every year, Efraín." Emelina looked at her husband, standing steady as he leaned his weight off the injury that hurt him. On the counter, Efraín had placed a bowl with an assorted variety of pears. She walked to the sink and ran water over the half-smoked cigarette. "Maybe it's time we start thinking about not going back," Emelina said, and reached for the fruit.

CONSUELO'S GARDEN

BEBA PLACED A DRY TOWEL AROUND Consuelo's shoulders, tucking the edge inside her housecoat collar. She squirted a dollop of hair gel into her palm, rubbed it gently through her friend's hair, and felt Consuelo's shoulders drop as she relaxed. Then, Beba wrapped short strands of hair around a plastic curler. It only took a few minutes and ten curlers to cover Consuelo's head. She had more pink scalp than white hair. The style wouldn't last more than a day, but Beba knew Consuelo looked forward to the Tuesday ritual that left her feeling pampered and pretty, or at least as pretty as she could feel at eighty with the left side of her face drooping from a stroke.

Beba rolled the last curler. "There, I'll blow dry it in a minute."

They had been next-door neighbors for forty years. Over decades, Beba and Consuelo had spent countless hours in one another's kitchen doing each other's hair, fashioning elaborate upsweeps like the telenovela stars, poufy perms, and countless frostings and dye jobs once they started to go gray. Now Beba came to the nursing home once a week and spent the day with Consuelo fixing her hair, giving her manicures, bringing her soups and smooth, syrupy flans.

Without turning around, Consuelo reached up for Beba's hands with her good one and said in her halting cadence since the stroke, "My ... house ... sold ... yesterday." She continued, slowly, pausing after every few words, "Diego called last night. The realtor girl said the offer was good. Except papers, it's done, my friend."

Beba sat down across from Consuelo. The elastic band of her navy pants made a snapping sound as she adjusted it around her thick waist. "Who bought it?"

"No sé . . . nada," Consuelo shook her headful of curlers. She dabbed the left corner of her mouth with a tissue because, she'd explained to Beba, she often had the sensation that the edge of her mouth was drooling, even though it wasn't.

"Bueno," Beba said. "I hope my new neighbors aren't—you know," she rubbed her index finger up and down her forearm.

Two months back, Consuelo, with the aid of her son, Diego, had put her house on the market. The stroke had weakened the left part of her body and taken away the use of her left hand. She couldn't live alone the way she had since her husband's death ten years back.

With Consuelo directing from her moss-green recliner in the living room, Beba had helped Diego sort through drawers, closets, and cabinets: things Consuelo wanted to take with her, things she wanted Diego to keep, things for charity, things that needed to be thrown away. And just like that, a fifty-year-old home ceased to exist. Empty rooms and bare walls.

"Are you sure Diego didn't tell you anything about who bought the house?" Beba asked again, because Consuelo now forgot things.

"No, he said ... the offer was good ... and the closing is Thursday." Consuelo reached out with her right hand and patted Beba's knee. "No te preocupes. It will ... be fine."

Beba drove past the front of Consuelo's house slowly before pulling into her own driveway. The *For Sale* sign now read *Sold* across it in bright red. The realtor must have done it while she was visiting Consuelo. Had she been home, she'd have walked over and asked about the buyers.

Beba hoped it wasn't the family with four kids. She didn't want that much noise. And, who can afford four kids these days? Irresponsible. And, not the couple with tattoos covering their arms and legs as if they were wrapped in comic strip pages. Por favor, didn't those people realize it made them look dirty and cheap? Beba wondered who else had come to last weekend's open house. She'd gone to Miami to visit her cousin, Estela. She could call Diego, but she didn't want to bother him. She knew he was busy. Consuelo said he was gone for work for a few days to one of those new states—Beba had trouble remembering which one—New York, New Jersey, New Hampshire.

The realtor's name was Cynthia, and the woman annoyed her. She hated the chirpy way she always greeted her and called her Miss Bee-bah even after she'd corrected her. *Beba like fella.* Was that so hard?

Beba always knew when Cynthia pulled into Consuelo's driveway because she gave her car horn three quick taps. The first time Beba heard the horn she thought she was being summoned and went outside. A superstitious habit for luck, Cynthia had said. *You know, the way baseball players have a routine before they bat. I want the house to know I want a homerun of a sale.* Qué jomerun ni qué carajo.

Beba walked to Consuelo's front yard. The towering royal poinciana in the center of the yard would bloom soon, ablaze with a canopy of bright orange flowers. She had a matching tree in her front yard. When the bloom petals fell, the lawns looked like they were covered with a dusting of orange snow. The trees had been saplings when she and Consuelo moved into the new subdivision built on what was then the eastern edge of Coquina Shores. Three bedrooms and one bathroom. Affordable. Dozens of Cuban families moved to the neighborhood. Many families were related, and she knew everyone. Now, many of those families were gone. Some had moved away to bigger, newer houses, and others sold when the elders, her contemporaries, passed away. Beba resented the way the neighborhood had changed. She hardly knew anyone anymore.

The soaring palm that grew at the right corner of the house was once a waist-high little thing Consuelo planted in memory of her father when he died in Cuba. Consuelo hoped her grief would diminish as the palm grew. They'd been neighbors for three years by then. Beba didn't care much for yard work, but Consuelo loved to garden. She'd filled the side yard with hibiscuses of every color, and frangipanis that bloomed pink and yellow. Beba knew Consuelo planted the cactus that grew by her bedroom window sometime in the early eighties when her husband Mateo strayed. He'd picked up with an old girlfriend who'd come over during the Mariel Boatlift. Consuelo said she'd worked too hard to build a life with Mateo to let some skinny-assed fletera take her man. She got rid of her with a strong trabajo.

Consuelo had bought a cow tongue and made a cut down the middle. She wrote Mateo and the woman's name on a piece of paper and tucked it in the middle, filled the fleshy crevice with black pepper corn and lemon rinds, then closed it with long sewing pins. Consuelo whispered an incantation to bring Mateo's union nothing but amargura y dolor—bitterness and pain. She slipped small pieces of cooked tongue into a beef stew she fed him and buried the rest outside their bedroom window. "You'll see," she'd said. "Their passion will rot with that tongue. And if traces of desire still linger, they'll have to make their way through the thorns of that cactus."

Beba was skeptical. But not six weeks later that woman packed up and left Coquina Shores for Miami.

She smiled at Consuelo's cactus. That thing had grown twelve feet tall. Mateo had never strayed again, and damn if that cactus didn't start giving red fruit and blooming twice a year with white, bell-shaped flowers.

The week had been filled with early Florida spring days with skies so clear and bright Beba felt she was living in a diamond. She opened her windows to the day's temperate weather. Spring was capricious in Florida, today's perfect open-window weather could change tomorrow to summer heat and humidity, or conversely, dip low enough to make a space heater necessary in her bedroom. Beba was making fideo soup for Consuelo. She was adding pasta nests to the chicken broth when she heard the metal-on-metal screech of truck brakes, followed by the hissing of a stop. If she looked out the living room window, she'd see a moving van in front of Consuelo's house, and she wasn't ready to stop thinking of it as Consuelo's house. The noodle nests uncoiled and expanded as Beba heard car and truck doors open and close. She stirred, careful not to overcook the fideos, squelching her desire to look out the living room window.

"Diego sold the house to un chino," Beba said to Consuelo. "What was our boy thinking?" She placed a bowl of soup on the rolling tabletop she'd positioned over Consuelo's lap. Beba draped a napkin bib-like on her friend's chest.

"He didn't . . . tell me . . . anything," Consuelo brought a spoonful of soup slowly to her lips.

"They're moving in today." Beba had a napkin ready in hand in case of spills. Consuelo refused to let her feed her.

"Qué rica . . . your sopa . . . my favorite. And?"

"No sé. I saw a woman giving orders to movers. And, an old man."

"We had chinos . . . lived on our street in Cuba." Consuelo continued slowly, "Well, he was . . . chino . . . she was mulata,"

"Bueno, at least this one is with a white woman."

The next day, Beba awakened long before she wanted to be up. There wasn't anything she needed to do, but she wasn't sleepy, and she wasn't tired. All those years she was working and raising her daughter, what she wouldn't have given to throw her alarm clock against the wall and go back to sleep. Now, she was her own personal alarm clock, awake early every morning for no good reason. She stretched from her side of the bed, warm from her body heat, to the cool empty side and ran her palm along the sheet. *Mi bella Beba, hora de brillar.* She could hear her husband's voice singing his silly rhyme, all the mornings he coaxed her awake. Almost five years ago she'd lost Daniel, and she missed him every day. Thirty-three since she'd lost Bebita, and she missed her daughter every minute.

Beba forced herself out of bed before she started feeling sorry for herself. Except for the achaques that came with age—coño, she'd be eighty-one soon—she was healthy. She kept that present in her thoughts as she lit the white candles she kept on her dresser for her husband and daughter. Beba lit a third one for Consuelo and began to pray a rosary for her friend. She'd looked pale last week.

Beba was lost in the trance-like repetition of Hail Marys when the clapping of boards startled her. She continued to whisper her prayers and walked to peek out her front door. Two men were unloading a trailer of fencing material in the driveway of Consuelo's house. Beba stepped out of the house, beads in hand, and saw the old man walk out and speak to workers who followed him to the side yard.

Even though it had been a week since they'd moved in, she hadn't met the neighbors yet. She kept her distance. You just never knew about people these days. She'd seen the woman leave in a silver SUV in the mornings. Off to work, Beba assumed. She hadn't figured out the man. She'd only seen him the first day. Maybe he was one of those old fools who married a young woman thinking it would make him younger—proof he still had what it took to be a man. That's why her cousin Estela's husband had left her six years ago. There he was, an old viejo chocheando acting like he was forty.

And la boba Estela, still waiting, foolishly hoping he'd come back. Maybe she should've done that cow tongue trabajo like Consuelo.

When the workers returned to the trailer for another load of materials, one of them touched the brim of his green cap in greeting. Beba returned inside. She went to her kitchen window where, through the gingham café curtains she'd sewn shortly after she and Daniel moved in, she saw the men preparing to work. A fence. A wooden fence between her house and Consuelo's.

Throughout the morning, the men dug holes and planted wheat-colored posts into the spring grass. Every pound and thud reverberated through Beba. She watched as the man who'd greeted her turned the brim of his hat backward and bent down, closing one eye and squinting the other, following the blue twine he'd staked along the length of Consuelo's side yard, making certain the fence posts were aligned. With each post, Beba grew angrier. This wasn't going to be an idyllic picket fence; it was a privacy fence that would shield her view of Consuelo's yard. As Beba's anger intensified, her footsteps became heavier; she closed drawers, cabinets, and doors with emphatic smacks. She slammed the refrigerator shut with such intensity that it shook, making the bottles inside clink.

In the late afternoon, after the workmen left, Beba sat in one of the wicker chairs outside her front door and kept watch for the silver SUV. She walked to the edge of her property, waving to the woman as she drove into Consuelo's driveway.

"I'm Beba," she said, introducing herself.

"Tamara."

They exchanged a handshake of sorts, briefly touching fingers.

"Just moved in and already making changes," Beba pointed to the fence construction.

"No time to waste," Tamara said.

The woman was thin and much taller than Beba. When she looked up at her, Beba saw dark swags beneath her eyes.

"My friend, Consuelo, lived here. She planted everything. I see her garden from my kitchen."

"Well, I guess the fence will change that, won't it? Nice to meet you, Beba."

Beba was left with her words in her mouth. This woman, this Tamara, turned around and walked away. Just like that. With nothing, no I'm sorry, no nada. Pero, qué cosa?

Consuelo was in bed propped up on pillows when Beba arrived on Tuesday.

"A bad night . . . my friend . . . a bad morning. I won't be . . . good company today."

"No jodas, vieja. You need me more on the bad days than the good ones." Beba kissed Consuelo's cheek. "So, no hairdo today. Nails? Are you hungry?"

Consuelo slightly shook her head to everything.

"What is it, Consi?"

"You know . . . when you don't feel bad . . . but you don't . . . feel right? Like that." Consuelo dabbed the corner of her mouth that sagged like the rim of a melting candle.

"Do you want me to leave so you can rest?"

"I want company."

"Is Diego back?" Beba said. "Has our boy returned from his trip?"

"Llegó anoche . . . late last night . . . he'll visit later . . . and, new neighbors?"

"The woman is called Tamara. I haven't met el chino." Beba didn't want to tell Consuelo about Tamara being cold and rude, nor about the fence. "The cactus is blooming," she lied.

"This . . . early?"

"Remember when you planted it with the cow tongue? How that trabajo worked!"

By the end of the week, Consuelo's house was boxed in by a six-foot high wooden fence that ran from each side of the house to the edge of the property lines and straight down to the back. When Beba looked out her kitchen window, she could only see the tops of the frangipani trees. They were in full leaf, but not yet budding.

The rapidity of the fence construction didn't surprise her. Florida. Beba had seen whole houses go up in weeks, and entire subdivisions developed in months. What stunned Beba when she came out of her house the day after the fence builders left, was the pile of plant debris at the end of Consuelo's driveway. Cut and piled one on top of the other, their roots ripped from the earth, were Consuelo's hibiscuses. The yellow, pink, and red flowers wilted, their stamens drooped pitifully.

Why do such a thing? Beba rang the familiar doorbell, once, twice, multiple times in succession, but neither Tamara nor the old man answered.

Consuelo was in the ICU at the Coquina Shores Hospital. Diego called as the sun rose and birds began their chatter. Cardiac arrest, he said. His voice sounded tired, worried, and young, even though he wasn't. Fifty-six, the same age as Bebita if she had lived. Fear can do that, Beba knew, bring out the child in us needing reassurance and comfort. Even at eighty, sometimes the only person Beba wanted was her mother. She'd longed for her when Bebita died. She'd ached for her mother's arms around her, knowing she'd never again put her arms around her daughter. She wanted her mother now. She wanted her to say Consuelo would be fine.

Consuelo was not fine. A machine with dancing lines beeped at her bedside. Fluids dripped into her veins, oxygen blew up her nose, and every few minutes a beast awakened, inhaling and exhaling loudly compressing her friend's legs. Beba touched Consuelo's forehead, smoothing her sparse, disheveled hair. Eyes closed, mouth crooked, bluish lips, gray age-mottled skin.

"She hasn't regained consciousness," Diego said.

She willed herself not to cry. "Take a break, mijo. Go home. Shower. I'll stay," she said.

Beba hated hospitals—hated this one in particular—where Daniel died after countless visits for the cancer that took him within a year. But worse, it was where she'd lost Bebita. In the emergency room right beneath her. The thin, gaunt Bebita she'd been unable to save. She'd overdosed weeks before her twenty-third birthday. The cocaine had been too pure. A life cut short and never-ending grief caused by purity. Beba whispered recovery encouragements to Consuelo and paced, praying her rosary. At Diego's insistence, she left the hospital mid-afternoon, exhausted.

When Beba drove up to her house, she saw Consuelo's cactus atop the pile of dead hibiscuses. Its thorny limbs amputated. Its trunk hacked to pieces. The tears Beba had kept in check at the hospital burst. What were they thinking? Beba rang Consuelo's doorbell repeatedly; she knocked on the door, then thumped on it with the palm of her hand, but she got no answer.

"You are killing her," Beba shouted in English and then in Spanish. "La están matando. Coño, me la están matando."

It was a clear night with an almost-full moon, and she was grateful. Beba waited until the houses on her street were quiet. No cars coming or going. No bedroom lights on, no televisions glowing through blinds or curtains. At the edge of her property, in front of the new fence, Beba bent her heavy body to her knees with some difficulty. She dug with a hand trowel, stabbing the ground, tearing apart the connecting roots of grass, exposing the sandy soil, breathing in the earth smell. The hole didn't need to be deep nor wide. She'd double wrapped the cow tongue in Publix bags. She'd filled it with pepper and lemon rinds the way she remembered Consuelo doing. On a yellow Post-it note Beba had written: *Tamara* and *El Chino*. She didn't know the words Consuelo used for her *trabajo*, but she knew how she'd felt. Now, Beba told the tongue her anger. She hated having Tamara and the chino living here. She hated the destruction they'd brought to Consuelo's garden. With every change they made, Consuelo became sicker. She wanted them to feel her pain. Beba spit into the hole, and filled it with dirt, burying her curse.

The following morning, Beba walked into Consuelo's hospital room expecting to find her better, but she was the same. Still unconscious, gray skin, blue lips dry and chapped. She seemed frailer, smaller, thinner. "You have to hang on," Beba whispered. "Give the tongue time to work." She dabbed Vaseline on Consuelo's lips. "You'll see." The beast roared awake, compressing Consuelo's legs. Inhaling, exhaling. Consuelo never moved.

Diego came to the hospital late in the afternoon after work. They'd agreed that Beba would come early in the morning to stay with Consuelo while he worked, then he'd take over through the night. Consuelo wouldn't be alone. He was a good son, Diego. Consuelo's one and only, her heart, just as Bebita had been hers. He'd never give her grandchildren, but he never failed her. And, Diego was alive. What Beba wouldn't give to have her child alive, regardless of her lifestyle. When Diego and Bebita were small and played together, before the darkness swallowed her daughter, Beba imagined them grown and married. She and Consuelo, comadres forever, doting on shared grandchildren.

All Beba wanted to do when she got home was have a hot cup of chamomile and take a steamy shower. The hospital was icy. She knew the cold controlled germs, but por Dios, she'd spent the day in a refrigerator. Her body ached. As she turned into her street, even from half a block away, she could see the mound of gravel. A pyramid of slate-gray rocks and a stack of lumber in front of Consuelo's garage. Y ahora qué? What the hell were they doing now? Again, Beba rang the doorbell, knocked on the door, and again there was no one home. Those people. She stood over the tongue, "Rot faster, por favor, rot faster."

For the third morning in a row, Beba left for the hospital shortly after the sun rose. The early morning sun glinted off the pile of rocks in Consuelo's driveway. They almost look pretty, she thought.

The frigid, antiseptic-smelling cold of the hospital made Beba shiver as she waited for the elevator to the ICU floor. Prepared, she slipped on her long, thick cardigan. Diego, haggard and unshaven, greeted her.

"No change," he said. "They're worried about stress on her kidneys. Maybe I should stay, but that project? The one from New Jersey? Tía, I need to have my design completed this week."

Diego was an architect. He designed big houses and buildings that, to Beba, always looked odd and futuristic.

"Go, mi cielo, I have her," Beba said. "You know, I always have her." Just like Consi had her when Bebita died. Back then it was Consuelo bringing her soup, coaxing her out of bed, convincing her that even though the grief would never leave her, she had to keep on living. For Daniel, Consuelo had said.

When Diego left, Beba took out the toiletry bag she'd brought. She dabbed Pond's face cream with the tip of her ring finger on Consuelo's face, careful of the oxygen tubes in her nose. She damped her fingers with Royal Violets and brushed Consuelo's hair away from her forehead. "Much better. Now you don't smell like hospital," she said. She wanted to tell Consuelo about the things in the driveway but didn't want to risk upsetting her. Instead, she told her the poincianas were beginning to blossom. Then Beba took out the rosewood rosary she used for holidays, funerals, and hospitals, inhaled the beads' perfume, and commenced praying.

When she got home after five, most of the lumber was gone from the driveway. Beba rang Consuelo's doorbell to no answer. Again, she pleaded with the buried tongue. The next several days followed the same pattern. Beba left for the hospital before the workers arrived, relieved Diego, sat with Consuelo, returned home to find the workers gone. She rang the doorbell, but no one answered; tried the side gates, but they were locked. Something with an unfinished roof had been built, but that was all that she could see over the fence.

By Friday, Consuelo was still unconscious. Diego returned after work, sat next to his mother's bed, looked up at Beba, and said, "The blueprints are finished. Sent. She's not getting better, Tía."

"It just needs time to work, mijo."

"What?"

"The . . . the rest, the care. You'll see. She'll get better. Have faith, mijo."

"Right." Diego ran his hand over his face. "I'm beat, and you're worn out. Go home, Tía Beba. Sleep. Sleep late tomorrow. I'll be here."

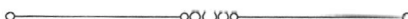

When Beba arrived home, Consuelo's driveway was cleared. No lumber. No rocks. A part of her wanted to knock on the door again, but she was exhausted—achy, stiff, sore—completely spent from the past week. She rested her forehead on her steering wheel, and whispered, "Work your magic, lengüita, work your magic, por favor." She crossed herself, kissed her thumb, and went inside.

The alarm clock was ringing. Beba murmured for Daniel to turn it off and reached out to him. Her brain engaged and she awakened, having slept deeply and long. The ringing started again, and Beba reached for the phone.

Consuelo was dead.

She pressed the doorbell and banged on the door at the same time. She had thrown on her cardigan over her nightdress, her feet in slippers. No answer. Dónde coño were these people? She banged on the door one last time before walking away. She stood over the buried tongue. Beba looked up and down the street. She spread her feet apart, took a deep breath to relax, and urinated. She felt the heat of her stream as some splattered on her legs. Malditos sean.

During the days that followed, Beba helped Diego choose the funeral flowers. She picked the memorial mass card, foregoing the traditional saints, crosses, and doves, selecting *The Heavenly Garden*: a paved path surrounded by blooming flowers leading up to the heavens. She picked out Consuelo's dress, and led the rosary at the velorio. She held Diego's hand as they rode the limousine to the cemetery and rested her head on his shoulder as they stood graveside.

Afterward, Diego took her home. She stood by her front door and raised a hand in farewell when he drove away. When his car turned at the end of the block, Beba walked next door and rang the doorbell in succession.

Beba was surprised when el chino opened the door. The knees of his khaki pants were stained with dirt. He was sweaty and had a smudge on his cheek.

"Do you speak English?" Beba crossed her arms.

"Of course, I speak English. My God, what's wrong?"

"She's dead, that's what's wrong. What did you do to her garden?"

"Who's dead? Should I call 9-1-1? How can I help?"

"It's too late." Beba covered her face and for the first time since learning of Consuelo's death, she began to sob.

He looked up and down the street, took her elbow and led her into the house. Assuring her that everything would be all right, he guided her through the living room, around the kitchen to the laundry room, and out the side door.

The side yard was completely different. The ground was covered with slate-gray gravel instead of grass. A serpentine trail of round white stones ran the length of the fence, stretching to the farthest end of the backyard and swirling to border the side of the house. A narrower swath of polished black stones followed the curves of white ones, separating them from the gravel. In the center of the yard, a square wooden deck had been built, covered by a lattice roof of thick crossbeams. By the deck, placed at three and nine o'clock, were square, gray brick planting beds filled with soil and perlite mixture with trays of assorted waxy succulents waiting to be planted.

He gestured to one of the wooden bench seats on the deck. "Sit, please. How can I help, Miss—?"

"Beba."

"Who's dead, Miss Beba?" he asked softly.

"My friend. This was her house."

"I'm very sorry. May I call someone for you, Miss Beba?"

"There's no one." She looked at him. Thick gray hair and black eyebrows, he wasn't as old as she'd thought. "A Chinese garden," she said, taking it in. "Because, you're Chinese."

He let out a sigh, ran his hand through his hair, and said, "No."

"Where are you from?"

"Delray Beach."

"No, I mean *where* are you from?"

"I was born in Miami. Jackson Memorial Hospital, to be exact. My parents moved to Delray when I was four. My mother was half-Japanese."

"And, this garden?"

"It's for my son."

"You and Tamara have a son? I haven't seen a boy."

"Are you sure there isn't someone I can call for you, Miss Beba?"

"Where is your boy?" Beba looked at him, "Bueno, where's your boy? This doesn't look like a good yard for playing. My friend's garden was good for playing. There was a swing set, back there, between the frangipani trees you cut down."

He shook his head, ran his hand through his hair again, and clapped his hands to his knees. "My son is not a boy, Miss Beba. He's a man, and Tamara is his wife. Her company transferred her here. He's still in Delray Beach. This garden is for him. There's a place in Delray Beach, the Morikami Japanese Gardens. Have you heard of them?"

Beba shook her head.

"Beautiful, sprawling gardens. My son loves them. He and my mother went there often together. Very peaceful, a place of calm and serenity. He's sick, my son, but he was getting better. Tamara needs this job, the health insurance, so we've been taking turns driving to Delray, and making this for him. A garden a little bit like the ones he loves, that he could enjoy as he regained his strength. But, he's gotten worse the last few weeks."

Beba shivered.

"I know it doesn't make sense, but I feel like if I finish this garden, my boy will get better."

Beba covered her face and wept.

"I'm sorry about your friend, Miss Beba. What was her name?"

"Consuelo," Beba whispered, "It means comfort."

HECTOR'S WOMAN

Gloria walked into La Media Noche bodega tired and hungry. She'd worked a double shift at the hotel because that woman Cindy, the one with the stringy red hair, called in saying her boy was sick. Gloria was grateful to pick up extra hours and the extra pay that came with them. But she'd spent fourteen hours changing sheets and squirting disinfectant on toilets. All she wanted now was a shower and some hot food. She could've picked up something quick at the Burger King or McDonald's but she wanted comfort food—something easy, something that reminded her of home.

Gloria bought a bag of yellow cornmeal, a head of garlic, some onions and a couple of beers. She paid with a twenty tucked in her uniform pocket and walked out the bodega door, its little bell clanging above her head, when a man's voice called out behind her.

"Señorita, you dropped this," he said extending a five-dollar bill and using the formal *usted*.

Gloria checked her pocket and, de verdad, the five that Chucho, the bodega owner, had handed her was missing. "Mil gracias," she said, and took the bill from the man's dirty hand. He wasn't unkempt-dirty; he was work-dirty. A chalky white film of dust from hanging drywall covered his body.

"Making harina?" He tipped his chin toward her grocery bag. "With lots of garlic and a good cold beer, nothing is better."

That night when Gloria poured the onions and garlic she'd sautéed in olive oil over her bowl of creamy, yellow grits, she envisioned the man's hands freshly washed.

She ran into him at La Media Noche the following week. They were checking out at the same time, and Chucho asked Gloria if she'd met Hector. He came from Pinar del Río, her province. Did she know that? Gloria said no; and Hector said the pleasure was his; and they traded names of long unseen places.

The first time Gloria invited Hector to her modest apartment for dinner she made ajiaco. She started the stew early in the morning, simmering the meats—beef, pork, chicken—and dense root vegetables. She waited, as she'd learned back home, until an hour before he arrived to add fleshy orange chunks of calabaza and pieces of plantains to the simmering pot so they wouldn't get mushy. Hector agreed that was how ajiaco was best. He saved the corn for last, sucking the stew juices from the chunks of cob. Gloria ate heartily too, with an appetite and satisfaction that came from not eating alone. Hector looked at her with food-sleepy eyes and said he couldn't remember the last time he'd been that content.

After dinner, Hector insisted on helping with the kitchen even though Gloria protested. He put on the black apron with *Domestic Goddess* spelled out in red rhinestones that she'd bought for only three dollars at Ross's, on sale since some of the stones were missing. While she divided the leftover ajiaco into two plastic containers, so he could take half home with him, Hector placed rinsed plates into the dishwasher. When the stew pot was empty, he scrubbed it while she put on the coffee. Making small talk as they worked, Gloria complained the kitchen smelled of old food no matter how hard she scrubbed. Hector used a table knife to unscrew the mesh filter underneath the stove fan. Gloria didn't know the filter was removable. He soaked it in detergent and it lost its grease smell.

Four months later, after many shared dinners, after Gloria knew how good Hector's clean hands felt on her body and how strong his thighs were when he pressed down on her, he moved in.

Gloria had been hesitant. At forty-eight, she'd had several men in her life, but she'd only lived with two: the young husband she'd married back in Cuba when she was twenty, only to lose him at twenty-three when his motorcycle was hit by a truck with faulty brakes, and the boyfriend she lived with for years but never married. She'd followed him to the United States. That one expected to be waited on hand and foot in the not-untypical Cuban way even though they both worked long days. He expected Gloria to serve him, clean up after him, and get up from the table to refill his water glass while they ate. She was used to that. But when he started openly keeping company with a long-legged Venezuelan and expecting her to look the other way, she put his clothes outside the front door and changed the locks.

When Gloria asked Hector about the women in his life, he said nobody special. He was stretched out on her couch with his head on her lap. Hector arched his head back for an upside-down kiss, and said, "Mami, I think I was waiting for you."

"No me digas," Gloria told him, letting him know it wasn't her first time around the block. Yet, Hector was different from most men she'd known. Hardworking, sure most of them had been, but Hector was helpful and tidy. He vacuumed without being asked, and more than once after a double shift, she'd arrived home to find him in her black apron, cooking. He picked up after himself, and sometimes after her. Three Saturdays ago, when Gloria couldn't find the flowy, gold-sequined top she liked to wear with black leggings for their occasional evenings out dancing at Luna's, Hector told her exactly where to find it: bottom left back corner of the bedroom closet hanging neatly.

One night in August, he sat on their bed fresh from his evening shower. Gloria took out the dirty laundry from the bedroom hamper. She took his work shirt and sniffed it. It smelled earthy and sweaty. Then, she reached down for a towel at the bottom of the hamper.

Gloria looked at the towel and looked at Hector.

He smiled, scooted onto the bed, and turned on the TV. His leg muscles flexed as he adjusted pillows and eased back. Gloria sat at the bed's edge. Above Hector's head were the shelves he'd built when he moved in. He'd worked in the short driveway cutting and sanding, running his palm up and down the wood until the smoothness met his satisfaction. He'd mounted them above the headboard. The shelves held back and white pictures of her long-dead parents, more recent color photographs of her sister and nieces still in Cuba, and a framed postcard of a bright green field dotted with patches of rich rust-brown earth leading to a ridge of rounded hills—the mogotes of the Viñales Valley in the province of Pinar del Río— the one place back home they both equally loved and missed.

Gloria sat at the bed's edge. "Are you cheating on me?"

"Ay, Mami, no. Why do you ask such a thing?"

He ran his finger from the curve of her shoulder to the tip of her chin and told her he loved her.

"Then, you tell me, whose lipstick is on this towel?"

Hector muted the television.

Gloria shook the beige hand towel at Hector.

Hector looked down at the remote in his hands. "Mine," he whispered, and a flush pricked his face.

"What?" The word squeaked out of her.

"I put makeup on sometimes. And other things."

"Cómo? Pero, qué tú dices? That you dress up like a woman?"

When Hector looked up and nodded, she knew he wasn't lying. His face had the same look that night when he explained softly over the phone to his mother that he couldn't get the arrangements made fast enough to go see her one last time, and Gloria knew he couldn't fake that.

"Do you like men?"

"No, I like women. And I love you."

"Do you *want* to be a woman?"

Hector shook his head.

"Then, why?" Gloria said.

"I like the way it makes me feel."

As television scenes changed behind her so did the light in the room. "I don't understand."

"I can't explain."

"Try, Hector. How does it make you feel?"

Hector took her hands in his and whispered, "It's like—it's like ajiaco, Gloria. It soothes me and leaves me content."

Gloria didn't let go of Hector's hands; she held them tightly. But she didn't know if she wished he'd just said yes. When she asked if he was cheating, she didn't know if she wished he'd just said yes.

The next day, as Gloria cleaned one hotel room after another, she couldn't stop thinking about Hector. Restless, she'd gotten out of bed in the middle of the night and typed "men who dress like women" in Spanish on her phone.

Travesti. She knew the word.

Gloria scrolled past various pictures of men dressed as women, to information. An article, written by someone in Argentina, explained that some heterosexual men found satisfaction wearing women's clothing. Gloria read the article slowly a second time to make sure she understood.

In another article, Gloria read about a woman whose husband dressed up as a man during the workweek and as a woman at home during weekends. On vacations, she helped him with his makeup, and they went out together. Gloria tried to picture Hector dressed as a woman but couldn't. The image that came to mind was of him, covered in fine drywall dust, as he'd been the first time she met him, but with lips painted in her deep red lipstick. Anxiety took hold of Gloria for the rest of the night, leaving her sleepless.

When Gloria entered their apartment after work, it was quiet.

"Hector?"

"En el cuarto," he said.

She followed his voice to their bedroom. Hector was in cargo shorts and tee shirt, with his hair wet from a shower. The dresser drawers were open, and he was placing neat stacks of clothes on the bed.

"What are you doing?"

Hector didn't look at her. "Packing, Gloria. Leaving."

"Why?"

"It's what people expect when they find out."

"What people?"

"First," Hector shrugged, "mi padre. He found me dressed up one day when I was seventeen. He came at me with fists and a belt. When he was finished, he kicked me out. He said if I ever let anybody find out, especially my mother, he'd kill me himself."

Because Hector didn't look at her as he spoke, Gloria walked around to the far side of the bed, in direct view of the stacks of clothing.

"Then, some guy I roomed with found me. He called me un maricón, and said if I didn't leave right then, he and his boys would break my legs."

"Ay, por Dios, that's just horrible."

Hector went to the dresser and returned with a handful of socks. "Besides them, only two other people have ever known. Alina, la cubanita I lived with for a while in West Tampa. She didn't even ask me to leave when she found out. She moved to her sister's place that same day. And now, you."

Gloria sat on their bed.

"You're a good woman, Gloria. I don't want to make you uncomfortable."

"Uncomfortable? I don't know that I am. I've never seen you, I mean, the other you."

"There's only one me."

"Then, let me see you."

Gloria gave Hector privacy in their bedroom. She emptied the dishwasher, then sat and thumbed through the latest issue of *People en Español*. She turned the pages without really looking at them, licked her index finger systematically, started again from the cover, gave up and flung the magazine to the far end of the couch. She picked up her phone and considered calling her sister in Cuba, but it wasn't Sunday, her scheduled day to call, and she didn't want to pretend everything was all right. She turned on the TV, remote in hand, changing channels. Gloria didn't want to think.

It was some time before Hector finally called. When Gloria opened the door. A ray from the late summer sun beamed in through the bedroom window. Dust particles floated in the air. Hector stood away from the window in the shadows of the far corner, head bowed, hands at his sides. He wore a red velvet V-necked sheath dress and sheer stockings with matching red heels.

"I . . . I keep some shoes and clothes in that locked box in the closet."

He'd said the box was personal. She'd thought he meant papers and photos.

He wasn't wearing a wig nor was he wearing a padded bra like she'd seen in some of the pictures she'd scrolled through last night. The velvet draped smoothly down his chest. The V-neck exposed some of his curly black chest hair. Gloria liked to draw fingertip circles there when they relaxed in bed, her head tucked under his chin. At first look, it was like seeing him dressed up for Halloween or a costume party. Gloria walked toward him.

"Look up at me, Hector."

As she'd imagined, he wore red lipstick. Foundation slightly covered the ever-present shadow of a beard on his freshly shaved face, and his eyes were rimmed in black. His makeup was applied flawlessly. This wasn't playacting. It wasn't the work of an amateur, and the realization startled her. Gloria looked up and down at Hector, saying nothing. She took another step closer, and in his face, she saw the same kind eyes and shy vulnerability she'd seen that first night at La Media Noche.

Gloria whispered, "You look, you look—nice."

Hector blushed.

"Y ahora qué? I mean, do you go out?"

He shook his head. "I'm very private," Hector whispered back. "I just want to be in my home."

"What do you do, tú sabes, when you dress and I'm not here?"

Hector took a step into the light. "I don't have many chances to be—alone. I watch TV. Just sit. Sometimes, I cook."

"Do you want to cook something for me?"

"I could make harina. The way you like it with onions and garlic. Do you think you can eat?"

"I don't know, Hector," Gloria said. "But I know I can try."

OLD CLOTHES

THE DINING ROOM WAS TROPICAL. GREEN rattan chairs with yellow floral cushions circled tables with white tablecloths. It had been one of the selling points when Olivia decided to move to The Glades Independent Living facility. She'd come to hate cooking just for herself after her husband died. Tall windows let in the Florida sunshine. Perfectly cheerful, Olivia thought. But then, Florida had commercialized aging and death for people of means. Hospitals had suites that rivaled luxury hotels, and funeral homes were painted soothing salmon pink. She considered herself fortunate.

The server, a young man about her grandson's age, handed her a menu.

"Waiting?"

"Just me. It's my first day."

He tapped at his name tag. "Anderson. Welcome, Mrs—?"

"Olivia Suárez."

"Would you like me to introduce you to anyone?" Anderson

poured her ice water and made a quarter-turn with the extended pitcher.

"No, no, thank you. I have reading to do." She patted a slim folder. She wanted to get a feel for the place. The young man nodded and walked away. He wore tiny gold stud earrings, dormilonas, they were called in Cuba. Often, newborn baby girls left the hospital with them in their ears. Her late husband, Eduardo, considered earrings on men effeminate—mariconerías, he called them. Olivia never admitted to him that she found them sexy. They conjured images of daring buccaneers, adventure, and open seas.

Olivia took out the monthly activities calendar. It was filled with choices: yoga, water aerobics, walking club, book club, card games, and movies. There were lectures on history and art. On Friday evenings, ice cream socials.

Olivia circled the socials.

The Glades had a bus that made daily runs to grocery stores, drug stores, and malls.

The loss of her ability to drive was one of the primary reasons she was there. She hated being cooped up at home all day just as much as she hated being dependent on her son, Eddie, or her daughter-in-law, Jessica. At seventy-nine, Olivia had chosen to give up driving. It was the prudent thing to do. Six months earlier, while driving out of her subdivision on a routine trip to Publix, a dog walked in front of her car. Olivia braked as quickly as she could, but she wasn't fast enough. It died on the pavement. Olivia anguished over the accident, but what haunted her was the thought that it could have been a child. A child. Of course, it could've happened to someone much younger. The dog was unexpected. But she knew her legs were stiff from arthritis, and her reaction time had slowed with age. She hadn't considered how diminished her abilities behind the wheel had become. She began hesitating in traffic. Doubting herself, Olivia couldn't drive without a wave of panic.

The decision to give up her car made her reevaluate other things. Her house, for one. Eduardo had died two years ago. The grandchildren who'd regularly filled the house were grown. They visited, but not for the extended stays common when they were little. Now, there were bedrooms Olivia entered only once a week to dust.

And then, there were her friends. Some had passed. Others, like her, lived routines. One day while having lunch with a friend, Olivia realized that during their every-other-Wednesday lunch dates they'd been having the same conversation for years. Olivia started considering her options.

She circled the art lectures on Tuesday mornings and the history lectures on Thursdays. She wanted to learn new things.

Three women entered the dining room. Their chatter and fluttery movements caught her attention, and she looked up as they passed.

"Mrs. Patterson?"

"Olivia?"

"Hello." Olivia nodded at the group. She hadn't seen Marjorie Patterson in over ten years. The last time was when she and Eduardo had run into Marjorie and her husband Gus as they left a movie theater. Gus Patterson had been a kind man. She'd heard he'd died five or six years back.

"What are you doing here?"

Olivia held up the circled calendar page. "I moved in yesterday." She said *yesterday* carefully, controlling her accent, so it wouldn't come out as *jess-tur-day*.

"Welcome," a tall woman with short, stylishly cut gray hair said. "You're going to love it here. Marjorie, introduce us to your friend. Have you ordered yet? How about we join you?"

The woman sat down without waiting for anyone to speak. "I'm Amanda, and this is Sarah."

With a soft pleased-to-meet-you, Sarah, a petite lady with fair, cinnamon-sprinkled skin, sat next to Amanda. Both turned to Marjorie, who remained standing.

Marjorie Patterson carefully tucked a strand of ash-blond hair behind her ear and sat down.

Se ha hecho trabajo, Olivia thought, she's definitely had work. Marjorie Patterson's face had that stiff, slightly shocked look that left her eyebrows too high up on her face.

With rapid-fire speech and a take-control attitude that made Olivia instantly like her, Amanda flagged over Anderson, ordered four mimosas, pointed at the calendar page and said, "Whatever you do, never miss the history lectures. That young professor that comes over from the university, well, first of all he's so yummy I want to eat him up, except he's young enough to be my grandson, which, ha, probably wouldn't stop me if he were interested, but seriously," Amanda stopped and actually took a breath. "He knows his stuff. Puts history in the right perspective, you know. What was going on socially, how women and minorities figured into it, you know, not the same old white men bull."

"Amanda's quite the activist," Sarah said.

"Always have been," Amanda said. "So, what about you, Olivia? You gotta jump right in hon. How do you know Marjorie?"

"Olivia Suárez," Marjorie Patterson said, "was my maid for years."

Her brother-in-law, Gabriel, followed a driveway lined by a neatly trimmed ixora hedge covered in coral-orange blooms to a house on the beach. Olivia breathed in the salt air and felt a pouring of homesickness wash over her even though she'd only been gone from Cuba for one week. Back in Las Palmeras, the whole town smelled of the sea. Eduardo started working construction within two days of their arrival. Through a friend of a friend, Gabriel found her a job as a maid.

"Scared?" Gabriel said.

Olivia nodded, "I know fourteen English words. I counted them this morning. How will I know what to do?"

"No te preocupes. I'll ask what they expect from you. Relax, you know how to keep a house."

Yes, she knew how to keep a house. She knew how to clean, cook, sew, and cross-stitch. Olivia knew because her mother had taught her. She'd raised a qualified wife. Her mother taught her how to make mirrors shine with vinegar-soaked newspapers and how to whip egg whites and sugar into silky meringues. She also taught her how to supervise the woman who came in weekdays to do the mopping, heavy cleaning, and laundry. It was one thing to run a house for one's family, it was another to have hands ruined by detergents and washboards.

Olivia had never had a job before. She'd been supported by her parents and then her husband. She never imagined she'd be anyone's servant. Olivia swallowed her pride and got out of her brother-in-law's car.

Marjorie Patterson answered the door wearing a pristine white tennis dress and a baby-blue headband that matched her eyes and frosted eye shadow.

Forty minutes later, Olivia was left alone with four bedrooms of unmade sheets and clothes-littered floors, three bathrooms that smelled of urine and a kitchen that was, surprisingly, clean.

Olivia found it disconcerting to enter her apartment and see her old things in a new setting. Even as he was helping her move in over the weekend, Eddie lobbied one last time for her to move in with Jessica and him. Her son was adamantly against her moving to The Glades. Sell the house? Sure, it was too much. He knew she got lonely, so why not move in with them? Because, Olivia explained, he and Jessica worked, and she'd be just as alone—different setting, same routine.

Olivia had felt just as disconcerted at lunch with Marjorie Patterson. She'd said her name out loud from surprise, not from a true desire to greet her. It hadn't been easy working for Mrs. Patterson. She was imperious and dismissive. She was impatient and habitually rolled her eyes if Olivia failed to understand.

Besides five boxes marked "fragile" stacked against a wall in the living room, Olivia's two-bedroom apartment was organized. Everything was unpacked except for her collection of Lladró figurines. She'd bought the first one on a trip to Spain with Eduardo twenty years ago, and he'd given her a new one for their anniversary every year after until his death. Olivia loved the pale subtle colors and delicateness of the porcelain. For his part, Eduardo was proud that he could spend hundreds of dollars on a piece. To him, it was proof of their success. While once his wife had spent two years collecting green stamps to buy a set of matching dishes for six, now she had an eight-hundred-dollar porcelain ballet dancer. As he grew older, the pieces began to matter more to him than they did to her. She'd considered selling them before moving, but it felt disloyal.

The lighted display cabinet for the Lladró pieces was a bit large for her new living room, but it still fit well enough. She'd sold or given away many furnishings, being selective about what to keep. At first, she'd thought it would be difficult getting rid of her possessions, mostly because of sentimentality. Coming from Cuba with only a few clothes had made the acquisition of things milestones. The first thing she and Eduardo purchased had been a full-size mattress. They slept with Eddie between them until they could buy a single one for him. When the time came to downsize her house, she felt less nostalgia than she'd anticipated. In the early years, every purchase led to saving for the next one: a couch, a dresser, a dining room table. Then she and Eduardo saved for better quality pieces. Now Olivia found that with everything she gave up, she felt freer.

Nothing but the clothes on your back and now look at you.

That's what chatty Amanda had said at lunch when Olivia gave her the compressed two-minute version of her history. Amanda's words were the same Olivia had heard for years when people learned she was once a refugee. She was proud of her history, but retelling her story had become tiresome.

"Marjorie," Amanda had said, "your friend is impressive."

Olivia wondered which word had irked Marjorie most—impressive or friend.

The white bus with The Glades sunrise logo rolled to a stop in front of the lobby doors as Olivia exited the elevator. It departed for the mall in fifteen minutes. Esto está de lo más bueno—she liked the idea of being chauffeured—door-to-door service with no parking worries. Olivia stopped at one of the lobby's mirrored columns. Her white hair coiled in a tidy French twist. Sometimes, if she caught her reflection in a mirror when she was distracted, she surprised herself for a fraction of a second. The old woman looking back at her was not the same as the woman in her head.

The mental image she carried of herself had frozen sometime in her mid-sixties. The woman in the mirrored column resembled her grandmother. Except that for the last twenty years of her life, her Abuela Severina had dressed in somber colors and never did anything more exciting than move from one shady spot on the terrace to another. Olivia smoothed down the front of her blouse. She'd bought several outfits before her move, cotton pants with colorful tops, clothes that were comfortable and young but age appropriate, stylish not ridiculous. She wanted the move to The Glades to feel like a beginning not an ending. She wanted to live more, not sit around and wait to die like her grandmother.

No one expected anything from her. She could do and be whatever she pleased.

Olivia sat in a window seat two rows behind the driver. A dozen men and women boarded the bus, some younger than she, some older, some moved slower than others. Olivia heard Amanda's laugh from outside the bus before she saw her. Then she saw her slap the driver's shoulder in greeting.

"Hola, anybody sitting with you?" Amanda didn't wait for a response before taking the empty aisle seat beside Olivia. Sarah followed behind Amanda, and then came Marjorie Patterson. They took the two empty seats across the aisle from Amanda, Sarah at the window and Marjorie at the end.

"Shopping and lunch," Amanda said. "We're trying out the new sushi place. Do you like sushi, Olivia?"

"Olivia likes to eat old clothes," Marjorie said elongating her o's. She tipped her head sideways and looked at Olivia.

"Marjorie, what on earth?" Sarah said.

"Yes, and so did Mr. Patterson. It's a dish—ropa vieja—shredded beef cooked with garlic, onions, peppers, capers, olives, tomato sauce." Olivia used her fingers to count off the ingredients. "You shred the meat after it's cooked. Old clothes are torn; that's where the name comes from."

"Sounds delicious," Amanda said.

"I'll make it for you. Saturday. Why don't you and Sarah come to dinner?"

"What about Marjorie?" Sarah asked.

"No, she always said old clothes were for peasants," Olivia said.

Olivia had been at the Patterson house for two weeks when Gus Patterson, through Gabriel, explained he wanted to increase Olivia's work hours. They were pleased; the house sparkled. Along with a raise would come an added responsibility: Olivia was to prepare dinner before leaving at five o'clock. The first day, Marjorie Patterson left out a plump chicken on the counter before heading out in her tennis whites. When Olivia asked "how," Marjorie shrugged and fanned her away. In the refrigerator, Olivia found onions, garlic, and a red pepper. In the pantry there were potatoes, cans of crushed tomatoes, and a well-stocked spice shelf. Olivia made sofrito for a fricassee. She simmered the chicken and potatoes in the tomato broth to which, at the final cooking stage, she added a bottle of Gus Patterson's beer. Shortly before Olivia left for the day, Marjorie Patterson arrived home with her daughters, followed by her husband. Although Olivia's English was still extremely limited, she now knew more than fourteen words, and little girls running to the kitchen saying *wow* needed no translation.

Gus Patterson respectfully patted Olivia on the shoulder with complementary good, good. Marjorie gave her a tight smile and a regal half nod. That was the thing Olivia found most trying during the time she spent working for Marjorie. She had no interest in the upkeep of her house, or in her kitchen, but there was an undercurrent of resentment that the person she hired to do the work for her succeeded.

One afternoon when she was fifteen or sixteen, Olivia came home from school to find Carolina, the woman who helped her mother with the house, placing Olivia's freshly ironed brown cotton Capri pants on her bed. "I know you like to wear them when it's your time of the month," she'd said. Olivia wondered how Carolina knew she was menstruating. Years later, after Oliva had spent two seasons under Marjorie Patterson's employment, she realized Carolina must have known many intimate details about her life, and that of her parents. Olivia knew when Marjorie Patterson used depilatory cream to remove the fine blond hairs from her upper lip. She knew the brand of condoms Marjorie's husband used and when he used them. Olivia smelled the musk of their lovemaking on their sheets.

Olivia became privy to her employers' habits. She also learned their strengths and weaknesses. Gus Patterson's strength was a perpetually pleasant disposition. He rose early to cook hearty breakfasts for his three yellow roses—that's what he called Marjorie and his two blond daughters—one six years old and the other eight, the year Olivia started at the Patterson's. She arrived at the house to find him in a red-checkered apron fixing plates of scrambled eggs and bacon or pancakes with blueberry faces. He cleaned up as he cooked, a habit, he said, from his Army days. Marjorie Patterson's strength was her ability to knead her compliant husband so that she always got her way. Her weakness was the inability to tolerate ever being upstaged.

There was one more thing about Marjorie Patterson that Olivia discovered some months into her employment. One she made certain Marjorie had no inkling that she'd noticed. Sometimes, when Marjorie left in her fresh tennis clothes and perfect makeup, her tennis bag and racket stayed tucked in the back of her closet, even though Marjorie always returned with a healthy glow.

The reading room at The Glades rivaled some libraries Olivia had seen. She arrived early for the history lecture. She wanted to look around on her own before other people arrived. Keeping with the tropical feel of the facility, the open room had light green carpet and lemon-yellow walls. There was a row of computers, and shelves full of books, both paper and audio, and DVDs. Stuffed armchairs in inviting groups circled low round tables.

In a rear corner, around one of the armchair groupings, a slender young man in black jeans and an untucked button-down plaid shirt was setting up padded folding chairs. With earbuds on, he kept rhythm with his head to whatever he was listening and silently mouthed the words. He turned, glancing up at the wall clock, saw Olivia, and smiled.

He removed one of his earbuds, finished unfolding a chair and greeted Olivia.

"Welcome. Are you one of the brave souls that's here to endure my talk today?"

Olivia nodded. "I hear you're very good."

"Bless you, glad to know I can continue to pay rent."

Amanda was right, he was handsome and charming. His name was Stuart, and he taught at the nearby university. He supplemented his income with lectures at The Glades. He was writing a book on Florida history, specifically, South Florida history. He and his girl-friend were driving all the way to Key West the following weekend because he needed to do some research, and she, a Michigan girl, had never experienced the long bridge drive from key to key.

After fifty years in this country, Olivia was still dumbfounded by how readily and unprompted Americans were to share personal information with complete strangers.

"Everyone should drive the bridges at least once," Oliva said.

"And the origin of that delightful accent, Miss Olivia?" Stuart said.

"Cuba."

Olivia had worked hard on her English and her pronunciation since her arrival. Even when exhausted after a full day dealing with the Patterson household, only to come home to deal with her own, Olivia diligently spent time every night with a grammar book. Then she invented other learning tactics. She often had the Patterson house to herself. Gus Patterson left for work after breakfast. Marjorie took the girls to school and left for tennis, luncheons, and other social activities. Olivia watched television as she folded laundry and ironed. She listened to the English, repeating the words to herself. She bought a small transistor radio, and made herself an apron with a pocket to hold it, listening whenever possible. Olivia made vocabulary lists and had the little Patterson girls repeat words for her. It was a mission for Olivia—she might be a servant, but she refused to sound uneducated. Her native Spanish was impeccable. No Cuban-swallowed word endings for her. She thanked her grandmother Severina for that. Her maternal grandmother arrived in Cuba from Castile, Spain, as a young bride and never lost her sibilant accent. Not once did she allow Olivia to drop her final syllables without instantly correcting her.

"Excellent," Stuart said. "My book deals extensively with the influx of Cubans to South Florida. Miss Olivia, I'd love to hear your story."

Before Olivia could recite her two-minute history speech, a group of residents entered the reading room, among them Amanda, Sarah, and Marjorie. Fifteen people or so filled the seating area Stuart had assembled. He greeted them by name and introduced Olivia. For her benefit, he explained that he usually had a topic, period, or event in history prepared to cover. The range of life experiences in his audience, he said, always provided lively discussion filled with personal anecdotes. Stuart said, he'd love for Olivia, if she felt comfortable, to tell her story.

She saw all eyes on her. She thanked Stuart, concentrating to say his name correctly so it wouldn't come out as Estuart. "My husband and I, with our two-year-old boy, left Cuba in 1966 on a Freedom Flight from Havana." She veered from her pat two-minute speech. Since her audience had come to hear a history talk, Olivia concentrated on the political situation that had prompted their decision to leave. Stuart spoke of Khrushchev and the Cold War. The audience listened attentively. A gentleman with golf clothes and a healthy tan half raised his hand, cleared his throat and said, "Excuse me, if this is impertinent, but I have to ask, how were you so successful that you ended up here? No disrespect, but we know this place ain't exactly cheap, and well, let's just say they don't give out scholarships here, do they? Know what I mean?"

Olivia heard uncomfortable laughs, and saw people readjust themselves in their seats, but what struck her were the expectant looks on faces. She realized Golf Man had asked what many of them wondered. From her seat at the end of the semi-circle, Olivia could see Marjorie directly across from her. Marjorie sat up straighter and looked right at her. Olivia averted her eyes from Marjorie and spoke to Golf Man.

"The early years were a struggle of course," Olivia said. "But with my help, my husband Eduardo started a business. A tile business—floors, bathrooms, kitchens. And, we were fortunate, the business grew. We expanded. Perhaps you've seen it? Gulf Tile and Flooring on North 41?"

"You did my marble floors!" a woman said.

"Did we? I hope you were pleased."

"Does your boy run the company?" Golf Man asked.

"No, we sold it when my husband retired. My son couldn't take over the company." Olivia looked right at Marjorie. "He's a doctor."

Eduardo had started painting houses for a construction company that built modest, single-family homes immediately after their arrival in Coquina Shores. The town was growing rapidly, keeping pace with the construction boom in the state. Soon, he started doing tile work that paid better. Eduardo, who'd managed his father's feed-supply warehouse before the revolution, was a quick learner and an ambitious worker. He bought an old van, some equipment, and started working for himself. Olivia continued at the Pattersons'. The income was solid and steady. While Olivia's English improved daily, Eduardo struggled with his. He taught her how to keep the books for the business. When customers wanted a job out of the ordinary or needed input on color or design, Olivia stepped in. Slowly, as word-of-mouth spread about the quality of Eduardo's work, projects for higher-end homes came his way.

Six years and two months after Olivia had started working for the Pattersons, she quit, giving them thirty days' notice. She and Eduardo had saved enough to open a small showroom and Olivia was going to run it.

Gus Patterson immediately offered her more money to stay.

"Thank you, but, no. Eduardo and I, we are very hopeful for the future," Olivia said.

While Gus Patterson expressed admiration for how much Olivia and her husband had accomplished, Marjorie said, "Olivia, I want you to replace all the shelf paper in the kitchen cabinets, and don't forget the pantry shelves. While you're at it, do all the bathroom cabinets as well before you go."

Golf Man came up to Olivia after Stuart's talk. He held out a large, open hand, and when she took it, he pumped her arm up and down. "I respect honest self-made people. They're the best kind."

Olivia squeezed his hand back firmly. She disliked men who shook her hand as if it were fragile as a bird, and she disliked women who shook back limply.

Several other people came up briefly to Olivia to introduce themselves and tell her they'd found her story interesting. When they moved on, Amanda and Sarah came up, too. Marjorie Patterson stayed slightly back.

"Good discussion, Olivia. Didn't I tell you Stuart put history in context? What time do you want us over Saturday? Is there anything I can bring? Besides wine, of course," Amanda said. "I see you met Steve, our golf champ—wins our tournament every year. Olivia's making us dinner Saturday. One of her signature Cuban dishes." Amanda took a breath.

Olivia felt slightly lightheaded. The morning lecture had turned into something she hadn't expected.

"Lucky you," Steve said to Amanda. "I love Cuban food. My son lives up in Tampa, and we go to The Columbia when I visit. Ever been to it, Olivia? In Ybor City?"

Of course she'd been to The Columbia, she even had their cookbook. She started to say so, when she realized something else was expected of her.

"Well, Esteve," Olivia was flustered, "please join us Saturday night."

Marjorie Patterson came up beside Steve. "Olivia, I think I've changed my mind. It's been so long since you've cooked for me."

"You two old pals?" Steve asked.

"Goodness," Sarah said quickly. "I think Olivia's generous offer is turning into a production. And, with her just having moved in. Olivia, please don't feel obligated."

"No, it's my pleasure to have you as my first guests in my new home. And, Marjorie," Olivia repeated the name slowly, "Marjorie, you're always welcome at *my* table."

Olivia dropped a bag of chamomile tea and a star anise pod in the boiling water and watched it turn amber. The flower-shaped pod danced circles in the water, swirling here and there, out of control as water bubbles popped. Olivia felt a bit like that after the history talk and its aftermath. Her first week at The Glades was more eventful than she ever imagined, and it was only Thursday. The aroma of chamomile, laced with the fragrant licorice scent of anise, rose from the water, instantly soothing her. It was a smell she associated with comfort. El cocimiento, as her grandmother called the tea, eased upset stomachs, menstrual cramps, sleepless nights, colicky babies, and unsettled nerves. She poured herself a mug and sat in her new living room.

She liked The Glades. The place was comfortable, lively and energetic. Amanda was funny, and Sarah was kind. What unsettled her was the unexpected presence of Marjorie Patterson. Y por qué? She wasn't ashamed of having been Marjorie Patterson's maid. She'd helped her family rise from nothing with that job. Had the circumstances been reversed, would Marjorie have been up to the challenge? The image of Marjorie cleaning her toilet made Olivia smile.

I think I've changed my mind. It's been so long since you've cooked for me.

She hadn't been invited in the first place. Marjorie Patterson considered it her right, her self-imposed privilege, to continue treating her as she did when she'd had to pick up her dirty underwear from the bathroom floor. The woman would continue to feel superior to Olivia and always treat her as she were beneath her.

How Marjorie Patterson felt about her was out of Olivia's control. How she treated her now was a completely different matter.

Olivia swallowed the last sips of tea and reached for her cell phone.

"Jessica, mi vida," she said to her daughter-in-law, "I know you're busy, but I need to run errands that will be difficult using The Glades' transportation. Could you drive me today or tomorrow?"

Olivia poured herself another cup of cocimiento.

Olivia set the table using the pale yellow-on-yellow embroidered tablecloth with matching napkins she'd bought on a trip to St. Martin. She'd arranged a bowl of low-cut red roses and daisies that accented the table without obstructing her guests' view of each other. She found it annoying when hosts placed large arrangements on dinner tables forcing guests to look around them peekaboo style in order to converse. She used her Lenox dishes and her good flatware.

On the coffee table Olivia set out a charcuterie tray of cured meats, cheeses, and olives she'd bought at the gourmet shop off Third Avenue. She turned the tray once, twice, adjusting it next to a stack of small colorful plates. On the way back to the kitchen, she stopped in front of the framed mirror that had hung in her foyer for years. She patted her twist to make certain no hairpins were loose and checked her teeth for lipstick. She shook her head. Ay, por Dios, she'd entertained countless times, but this time it had to be perfect.

Olivia took out of the refrigerator a container of sliced oranges and lemons she'd soaked overnight in sugar and brandy. She poured some in a sangría pitcher, adding red wine and seltzer. Bless Jessica, she thought. She couldn't have gone to the gourmet shop, the florist, the liquor store, and the grocery store without her help.

When the doorbell rang, Olivia stood still. Americans! Right on time. She took a deep breath, counted to five slowly, and opened the door.

Amanda entered first, joyous and exuberant as Olivia had come to expect even though she'd only known her a few days. She handed Olivia a bottle of wine, as did Steve and Marjorie. Sarah presented Olivia with a fabric-covered notebook.

"It's a guest book for your new home. They can write something about their visit. I have one at my place. I keep it in the bathroom—it's my little joke."

"Well, thank you. You can make the first entry later." Olivia found the image of her guests writing in her bathroom peculiar. She placed the notebook and wines on the narrow entry table beneath the mirror. "I'm happy to open wine, but I've made sangría."

"Homemade sangría?" Steve asked.

"My grandmother's recipe. She was from Spain."

"I won't pass that up."

Amanda and Sarah agreed; Marjorie acquiesced with a barely perceptible chin nod. Olivia ushered her guests around the coffee table. She joined them with a tray of glasses and the pitcher of sangría.

She spoke as she poured, handing Marjorie her glass last. "My grandmother Severina, on my mother's side, emigrated from Spain to Cuba. She was from Castile in Northern Spain. Beautiful country. My husband Eduardo and I visited years ago. Have any of you been?" Olivia purposely didn't wait for an answer. "A toast. To new beginnings."

She passed out hors d'oeuvres plates. Again, handing Marjorie hers last.

"My grandfather was a merchant of sorts, an importer. He traveled back and forth from Cuba to Spain bringing back Spanish goods that were in demand on the island. Olive oils and olives, like these. Try them, they're delicious." Olivia pointed to the charcuterie plate and took a sip from her glass. "That's manchego cheese. It's made from sheep's milk and originates from the La Mancha region. I call it quixotic cheese, but that's just my little joke." Olivia concentrated hard as she said *joke*, so it didn't sound like *yoke*, and winked at Sarah.

"Oh, I get it," Sarah said.

"Was your father an importer as well?" Amanda asked.

"No, he owned ranch land. A modest ranch, comparatively espeaking." Concho, she was so focused on using *comparatively* correctly, she flubbed the beginning of *speaking*. After all these years, beginning S's and J's still gave her trouble. "Three thousand hectares, in acres that's—"

"Oh, seven thousand three hundred and fifty," Amanda smiled, and blew on the tips of her fingers, rubbing them on her shoulder. "Math major in a former life."

"That's not nothing, Olivia," said Steve. "Damn good sangría. Your grandmother knew her stuff."

"I made plenty," Olivia reached for the pitcher. "My father's land was expropriated shortly after the revolution."

"Expropriated?" Sarah asked.

"Confiscated," Amanda explained. "Taken by the government."

"Just taken?"

"Yes, Sarah. My parents were permitted to keep the house, which was modest. The value was in the land. Raising cattle requires a lot of acreage. My father died not long after that. The doctors said it was his heart, but my mother believed it was his spirit. It was broken."

"And your mother?" Sarah asked.

"She was supposed to come with us—with Eduardo and my son—but, well, my father's death was hard on her. She wasn't strong. She died before our leave out of Cuba was granted."

"How is it I never knew any of this?" Marjorie spoke for the first time since arriving.

"You never asked," Olivia said.

"And how is it that you two know each other?" Steve mimicked the tone in Marjorie's voice.

"What? She hasn't told you? She couldn't wait to tell these ladies right away. When I first came to this country, I was Marjorie's maid."

Steve coughed on the bite of manchego cheese he'd just taken. He took a gulp of sangría and pointed. "You, Miss Olivia, were Marjorie Patterson's maid?"

"Maid, housekeeper, cook. We came with nothing. I started work right away."

The man threw his head back in laughter and slapped his thigh. "That's rich. This lady here, fresh off the boat, Marjorie, was your maid."

"She said she came on a plane," Marjorie said.

Steve laughed so hard his eyes watered. Either out of contagion or embarrassment, Amanda and Sarah laughed, too.

Olivia joined in. "The world is curious, isn't it?" she said.

"So, what kind of a boss was Marjorie, Olivia? Was she persnickety?" Amanda said.

"Oh, for Pete's sake. I thought we were here for Cuban food, not history lessons. We had enough of that Thursday." Marjorie tucked a strand of hair behind her ear.

"Yes, my old clothes," Olivia elongated her vowels. "I have rice, salad, Cuban bread, and flan for dessert."

Her guests ate with gusto, except for Marjorie who picked at her food. Olivia kept the sangría flowing, mixing a second pitcher.

"What a feast," Sarah said.

"Olivia, you never answered my question," Amanda said.

"Which question?"

"Was Marjorie here, a persnickety boss? You know, picky, fussy, difficult?"

"Really, Amanda!" Marjorie said.

"I'll always be grateful to the Pattersons for taking a chance on me. I was very lucky to find a job—not having any work experience—not speaking English. Marjorie's husband taught me how to make the best pancakes! He made breakfast every day for the family. I remember, Marjorie hated the kitchen. Loved tennis. Played all the time. Sometimes she was so excited to get to her games, she'd forget her racket. You know, it's such a personal relationship. Why, the intimate details you learn about people! We had help at our home when I was growing up, and my mother always said, reliability and discretion were very important, yes? Nobody wants someone talking about their old clothes around town."

"You mean their dirty laundry," Amanda said.

"Dirty laundry. Yes, that's how you call the things you don't want talked about." Olivia laughed. "Dirty laundry. Let's sit in the living room for dessert. I'll make coffee."

Sarah picked up her plate.

"No, no. Just leave that, Sarah, let's continue our conversation."

Olivia looked directly at Marjorie.

"That's an impressive collection of Lladró pieces, Olivia," Marjorie said. "I have a friend that collects as well. Maybe next time she visits, you'd like to meet?"

When the Sunday morning light was so bright that it penetrated Olivia's thick bedroom curtains, she finally forced herself out of bed. The work she'd put into the previous evening, plus the anxiety that had come with it, left her exhausted. Olivia mustered enough energy to transfer herself from her bed to her couch with a cup of café con leche. It was already mid-morning. Jessica called at noon for a report on the evening. Successful, she said, perfectly successful. Another cup of coffee, toast, a little TV; it was three o'clock when Olivia decided to shower and change from one set of pajamas to another.

By Monday morning, Olivia felt normal and pleased with herself. In the dining room, young Anderson handed her a breakfast menu.

"Mrs. Suárez, how was your first week?" He filled her glass with water.

"A challenge, Anderson, a tiring but successful challenge."

"Awesome. Coffee? Or would you like to celebrate your success with a mimosa?" Anderson tilted his head and gave her a smile. He reminded her of her grandchildren when they were small, trying to convince her to let them eat cookies for breakfast.

"Just coffee. I had a lot of sangría Saturday night."

"Way to go, Mrs. Suárez."

Olivia laughed. "I like your earrings, Anderson."

"Thanks. My father hates them."

"My husband would've hated them, too." She'd wanted to get her ears double-pierced back in the 80s when it first became popular, but Eduardo wouldn't let her. He thought double piercings made a woman look cheap. But Eduardo was dead.

"Where did you get your ears pierced, Anderson?"

DRESSING THE SAINTS

CARMELA PUT THE PERCOLATOR ON THE burner and turned it on high. While the coffee brewed, she leaned against the sink, looked out the kitchen window at the blood-red bougainvillea covering the back fence, and waited for her morning are-you-alive visit. Carmela knew that Delia, may she rest in peace, would be delighted that her bougainvillea still bloomed season after season. She missed her sister-in-law every day.

When the coffee was ready, Carmela poured a cup and added two spoons of raw brown cane sugar. The slight uncontrollable tremble of her hand sloshed coffee over the brim as she stirred. She took her first sip and placed a slice of Cuban bread in the toaster. The microwave clock glowed ten past eight. When the toast popped, Carmela dunked it in the coffee and gummed the sweet, wet bread. She hated wearing her teeth first thing in the morning.

Halfway through the toast, the doorbell rang, and Carmela called, "I'm coming."

It took time to get to the door; her joints hadn't warmed up yet to the day. Out of habit, she drew back the living room curtains. Her niece checked in on her every morning before work and telephoned in the evenings after Carmela was done watching the telenovelas. Her brother and Delia had raised a good woman. Carmela peeked around the gauzy material and caught her breath. Luisa was at the door as expected, but so was Maggie.

She opened the door and clapped her hands in delight, "Look who is here!" Carmela wrapped her arms around Maggie. Her beautiful grandniece was the living image of Delia. Maggie had her grandmother's compact, efficient body, and her thick, black eyebrows—one arching higher than the other—over the same round, light green eyes.

"When did you get here?"

"Late last night, Tía." Maggie hugged Carmela gently.

"She says she's between projects and showed up last night." Luisa made her way around Carmela into the house. "Didn't call, all alone on the road, wanted it to be a surprise. Sí, imagine the surprise if something happened, and some policeman comes to tell me because she wanted to surprise me."

"Ay, Mami, please, don't be so dramatic. One, I was perfectly safe. Two, I drive alone all over the state, and yes, oh, my God, even *at night*. And three, I have a cell phone. Tía, do I smell coffee? You know your coffee is my favorite."

Maggie made her way to the kitchen and Carmela followed. "Sit down, Tía, I have it." Maggie took two small coffee cups from the cabinet, poured the still-hot Cuban coffee in them, and refilled Carmela's cup.

"How'd you sleep, Tía Carmela? How's your hip?" Luisa asked.

"It's fine. I'm fine. And before you ask, yes, I took all my pills this morning. Maggie, this mother of yours takes such good care of me. I don't know what I would do without her."

"You'd do better if you listened. Last week, this old woman gets up on a step ladder to wash the windows and—"

"Ay, por Dios, I was only two steps up, and if I don't Windex the outside of the kitchen window, how am I going to see the backyard from the sink. Did you see the bougainvillea?"

"Two steps up? You're ninety-one. You shouldn't be any steps up at all. And this one, driving across the state after dark. Thirty-four and no husband. Left to dress the saints. Do either one of you listen, pués no. I'm late for work."

"Poor Luisa—have you heard?" Maggie shielded one side of her mouth as if telling a secret. "Her youngest is a spinster. Luisa couldn't get that Maggie married, and she's late for work."

"That's not funny."

"Why don't you retire already, Mami?"

"Ay, please, like that place could run without me. I have to go."

"Are you both leaving?" Carmela asked.

"No, Tía, I brought my car. I came to spend the day—unless you have a hot date?"

Carmela covered her toothless mouth with her hand. "Ay, Maggie, the things you say. Just like your grandmother. Isn't she, Luisa? Isn't she just like Delia?"

Luisa took a breath, adjusted her skirt over her ample thighs, and nodded. "You two behave, and Tía, put your teeth in."

When her niece closed the front door, Carmela said, "And she doesn't understand why I won't move in with her. She is very good to me, your mother, but qué majadera. My God, she thinks the world can't run without her."

"How are you, really, Tía Carmela?" Maggie asked.

"At my age, if I can wake up and get out of bed, I'm fine. How are you? Tell me what you've been up to."

Maggie did something with computers that Carmela didn't quite understand, but she knew her grandniece worked for a company that sent her to different cities around the state. She stayed four, six, eight weeks at a time in these places, and Carmela received postcards from all over Florida—one was from a town called Sebring—Carmela hadn't heard of that place until the postcard arrived. Maggie's home office was in Fort Lauderdale, where she lived and owned an apartment. Carmela used the words when she spoke with Maggie so that her grandniece knew she cared and paid attention. She'd ask, "How is your home office?"

She loved when Maggie visited. Sometimes, she'd show up at Carmela's door and proclaim they were going to play *Júqui*. The first time Maggie showed up to play *Júqui*, Carmela figured it was a board game like Parcheesi or Monopoly, but Maggie laughed and said no. When Maggie laughed, Carmela heard Delia. Carmela loved *Júqui* days the best. They went to the pier and to parks; they ate lunch in little restaurants. They went to the mall and to the movies. Her English wasn't the best, but Maggie always told her about the story before the film started, so she could follow along. She liked action movies where there were guns and car chases and lots of things blew up. They were exciting, and it didn't matter that she didn't understand all the English.

"I'm between projects, like Mami said. I'll be working at the home office for, well, for a while. The drive was easy; there's no traffic at night. And, I know it's a pretty day, but, if you don't mind, I thought instead of playing hooky, we'd just stay here today?"

Carmela was disappointed, but she gave Maggie a toothless smile. "Of course not, mija. You look tired. Sit and rest. I'll go fix myself up." Carmela patted Maggie's hand.

Carmela slipped on loose cotton pants and a blouse, ran a comb through her closely cropped gray hair, and put in her teeth. She chomped her jaw up and down to set them in place and licked the minty enamel. Before leaving her bedroom, she dabbed Royal

Violets on her wrists and temples.

Maggie wasn't at the dining room table. Carmela looked out the kitchen window to the backyard and saw her on one of the chaises. She took the plastic container of bird seed out of the pantry and walked out to join her.

"Here you are. The birds eat the seeds faster than I can fill the feeder."

"It's always nice back here," Maggie said. "Peaceful."

"See the avocados and mangoes coming in?" Carmela pointed at the trees on opposite corners of the yard. "And—"

"And the avocado tree is as old as me," Maggie said.

"How did you know I was going to say that?"

"Because you always do. Abuela Delia planted trees for each person in the family, and the avocado tree is me."

Carmela sat in a separate chaise alongside Maggie.

"Are you lonely here all by yourself, Tía?"

"Everybody gets lonely sometimes, mija, even when they have people around. But I'm comfortable, in my own home, and as you said—it's peaceful."

Carmela had lived there for fifty years, but it hadn't always been her *own* home; it had been her younger brother's. In Cuba, she'd stayed in her parents' home well into adulthood, as was customary for daughters who didn't marry. Her mother died, and then her father. She'd lived alone in her childhood home for less than two years before leaving Cuba in 1966. Carmela was forty years old. She left with her brother, Delia, and ten-year-old Luisa on a Freedom Flight. They came to live in Coquina Shores because Delia had cousins here. That's the way it was in the new country; one relative followed another. This house had one bedroom for her brother and sister-in-law, one bedroom for Luisa, and one bedroom for her.

Carmela looked at Maggie. She'd slid down on the chaise, and was stretched out flat, only her head leaning on the back support. Maggie was healthy and fit, in black workout shorts, a green T-shirt, and bare feet that she'd slid out of her sandals. Her grand-niece's black hair was cropped short like hers, except Maggie had a wide strand dyed bright red that crossed her head, swooped across her forehead, and tucked behind her right ear. Carmela couldn't remember ever looking or feeling that young. In her day, a somber-ness was expected of women after it was clear they wouldn't marry. With no man or children of their own, they were left to dress the saints—volunteering at the church, polishing the faces and chang-ing the gowns of the virgins.

"Your mother should not have said that to you today," Carmela said.

"Said what?"

"About you dressing saints. You have such a life, mija. Working, traveling, you have your own home. One you chose for yourself."

"I didn't follow Mami's expectations. I'm not like my sisters."

"I've always known life held something different for you, Maggie."

Maggie rolled sideways on the chaise toward Carmela and propped her chin on her hand. "Why didn't you get married, Tía?"

"Life held something different for me, too, mija."

"Were you ever in love?"

A flush rose from Carmela's chest, warming her neck, tightening her scalp into prickles, pressuring the back of her eyes.

"Tía, you were in love, weren't you? I can't believe in all this time I've never asked you. What happened?"

"Ay, Maggie. It worked out differently than I expected."

"What do you mean?"

"Why all the questions?"

Maggie sat up and shook her head. "Well, bueno, because I never thought to ask you. It never came up. And now it has and, I need, I'd really like to know."

Carmela picked up the bird seed container and walked to the feeder that hung from a bottle-brush tree. "It is all in the past. There's nothing you need to know. I will tell you one thing. I was loved back."

Maggie followed Carmela and took the seeds from her. "Here, let me do this. There is something I *do* need you to know."

Maggie held the container with one hand and reached for Carmela's hand with the other. "I'm loved back, too."

Carmela closed her hands over Maggie's. "Ay, mija. This is wonderful news. It's a good thing! Tell me all about it."

"Yeah, it is good." Maggie poured seeds quickly into the bottom of the green wooden house bird feeder. "Let's sit down again, Tía. I need to sit down."

Carmela let Maggie curl her arm around hers as they walked back to the chaises and wondered who was helping whom.

"Maggie, niña, are you all right?"

"Just tired." Maggie sat in the lawn chair and reached for Carmela's hands.

"Bueno, vamos, tell me all about this new love."

"Actually, it's not so new."

Carmela nodded. "Ah."

"Tía, it's not like, well, like it was with my sisters."

"I know, Maggie."

"No, Tía, you don't. You don't understand."

"Ay, Maggie, I understand better than you'll ever know, and I'm feeling very, very old. What's her name?"

Maggie stood up and walked behind the chaise, holding the top of the backrest as if for support. "You know? How long have you known?"

Carmela held up her hands. "I think I've always known."

"Why didn't you tell?"

Carmela shook her head. "It wasn't my place. It was for you to tell if you wanted. I feel so old, Maggie. I want you to know I love you for everything you are."

Maggie made a low sound that was part laugh and part moan. It came out of her, growing louder, and turned into a wail. Maggie sobbed. Carmela knew those kinds of tears. They were the held-in ones that grew unbearably heavy with time.

Carmela rose, and put her arms around her grandniece. "Breathe, child. Come sit, sit and breathe. Do you want water?"

Maggie shook her head, sat next to Carmela, and buried her face into her shoulder. She held the girl until her crying slowed.

"Does the rest of the family know?" Maggie sat up. "Oh, my God. And, Mami going on about how I wouldn't find a husband. All that pretending. For nothing? I moved away because I couldn't be myself in this town. Not without disappointing everybody. You know how Mami is. Does she know, Tía? Does the family? Have we just been playing a stupid game?"

"Listen to me, Maggie. As for your two sisters? Who knows? I've never heard them say anything."

Maggie tucked her red streak behind her ear.

Carmela drew a deep breath and exhaled. "You know I love your mother as if she were my own daughter. I helped raise her, and I don't know how I'd get by now without her. But she's too much like my brother, that one. Too concerned about appearances and what people think, for one thing, and strong willed. You get *that* from them. Domineering, the both of them." Carmela let out a laugh. "Even your own father doesn't know what to think unless Luisa tells him."

"Poor Papi." Maggie shook her head and her red streak came loose again. "She does nag him."

"Luisa sees the world the way she wants to see it. Just like my brother. If I had to bet this house, I think deep down, she knows why there was never a man for you. But that's not what she chooses to believe."

"So we have been playing a game."

"No. You've been living life. Have you been happy? Have you been content?" Carmela saw Maggie give a nod and continued. "Your mother has done the same."

"I'm about to make her very unhappy."

"Your new love that's not so new?"

"Susan. I met her three years ago. Remember when I spent two months working in Sebring? She lived there. She's been out for a long time. Do you know what that means?"

Carmela slapped her knees, "Mija, like Celia Cruz used to say, 'my English is not very good-looking,' but I know what that means."

"Okay, so okay. Well, she moved to Fort Lauderdale a year ago, in together with me. She's wanted me to just tell the family, and now," Maggie shook her head.

"And now what, Maggie? Now, you've told me? Niña, I would

never betray your trust."

"Oh, no, por Dios, I know that. No, no. It's just that now," Maggie rubbed her closed eyes with thumb and index finger.

"Remember I'm old, Maggie. I could die before you finish the sentence."

Her niece looked directly at her. "Tía Carmela, I'm pregnant. Susan and I want to have a family, so I got artificially inseminated. It worked the first time. That's rare, Tía. It's like it was meant to be. It worked the very first time."

Carmela covered her mouth with both hands.

"I hoped that with a baby coming—I hoped Mami and the family would just be happy for us."

Carmela placed her hands on her heart, and felt her eyes fill up. She remembered the day Delia told her she was pregnant with Luisa.

"Say something, Tía, please say something."

"Ay, Maggie, no wonder you're so tired."

Maggie left mid-afternoon to go speak with her mother alone after work. Carmela went inside, poured herself a glass of sherry, and returned to the chaise. She prayed Luisa would be reasonable. The sherry was an indulgence. The day called for commemoration. She raised her glass and toasted it and the backyard. An avocado tree can take years to mature and bear fruit. Delia had chosen wisely for Maggie.

Carmela hadn't lied to Maggie. She had been deeply in love. And, it hadn't turned out as she expected. That was true, too.

She'd fallen in love with Delia the first day her brother brought her home to meet their family. Beautiful, kind, intelligent Delia captured her heart the same way she'd captured her brother's.

Carmela had no options on the island. Unlike Maggie, she couldn't go away to live her own life. She'd permitted suitors to come calling simply to appease her parents and for the sake of appearances. She'd fought with her loneliness and cried her own heavy tears. Carmela had resigned herself to living quietly with her parents and caring for them in their old age. Nothing else was expected of her.

Then the revolution came. Her mother died of cancer, and her father of a weak heart. Carmela found herself on a plane bound for a new country with her brother and the woman she loved. She helped Delia raise her daughter, cook meals, and keep house. Untrained to work outside the home, but needing jobs, they worked side by side in a hotel laundry washing and folding mountains of sheets and towels.

Her brother inherited their father's weak heart. He died sooner than anyone expected. She and Delia shared their grief. They were companions and confidantes. Carmela never told Delia how she felt. To do so would have served no purpose. She loved Delia and Delia had loved her back. She knew it wasn't the same as what

Maggie shared with Susan, but it was more than she'd ever expected.

Carmela focused her eyes on the fiery red bougainvillea that Delia had planted for her, sipped the sherry, and felt it warm her.

HARBOR PILOT

ALBERTO STEPPED INTO LA CONCHITA BAKERY and paused just inside the door. He blinked a few times to help his eyes adjust from the Florida sunlight, and inhaled the doughy, sugary-sweetness. He took off his boat captain's cap and brushed his hand through his thin, white hair.

"Alberto." Conchita greeted him from behind her glass counter. "What do you wish this fine day?"

Alberto favored his right leg walking toward her. Fifty years later, the bullet injury still bothered him. With his arthritis getting worse, he swayed from side to side as he approached the counter.

"My wish is to see your face, the sweetest among the sweets."

"Ay, viejo, nice piropo, but that line is as weak as your leg and just as old. How are you today, my friend? What can I get for you?"

"I'm alive and walking, Conchita. That's as good as it gets at eighty-two, no? Pastelitos de guayaba, señora, two dozen."

"You having a party?"

"Albertico got home last night. We meet his girlfriend's family today. They are driving from Miami."

"How is that grandson of yours? I thought he was still in Gainesville."

"Sí, sí, he is. The girlfriend and the family? Cubanos de Miami. Such is destiny. The boy leaves Coquina Shores for the University of Florida and meets a decent Cuban girl. They graduate this year. And, our Albertico, his degree cost him almost nothing, because he is so smart. He is a *meriescolar*. And when you are one of those, one of those *meriescolar*, they pay for your university."

"So you've said, viejo, so you've said." Conchita put the last guava pastry in the box and closed the lid. "Congratulations to you and your family. Twenty-seven pastelitos, señor. Enjoy."

"Twenty-seven?"

"Pués sí. One free for each dozen, and an extra one for your piropo. It's the only compliment I'll get all day—qué coño, all week."

Alberto placed the pastry box on his truck seat next to the two bottles of Anís del Mono, the sweet kind, he'd bought at ABC Liquors: one bottle to open with Yadira's family to honor the visit, and one bottle to give her father as a gift. He'd given his father-in-law a bottle the first evening he went courting. His Violeta, six years gone now. He gave Rogelio a bottle when he granted him his Clarita's hand in marriage. A small tradition of his own making.

This would show Yadira's family that their Albertico came from good people.

Alberto drove home the roundabout way. He took 41 to the Four Corners and took a left where the highway turns south and crosses the river as it empties into the bay. Most days, but especially on warm days, the fishy, woodsy smell of the brackish water wafted over the bridge. He always opened his truck windows and stuck his head out, savoring it, like a dog on a drive. Alberto liked to see the boats at the marina. Recreational boats. No cargo ships nor barges. The days of taking his small Boston Whaler out alone were gone, and he missed the water.

The family was right. Just too old now to go out alone. Driving his truck he could still do, but only in the daytime. To the bakery, to la bodeguita, Home Depot, and Publix. Places he knew well. But his night vision was terrible, and the water, pa' qué decir, the water was just too unpredictable.

Alberto walked into his daughter's house, his home now, too, and gently pushed the front door closed with the side of his good leg. He stood in the foyer, ABC bag in one hand, and the box of pastries in the other. The foyer opened to the living room and beyond that, through sliding glass windows to a sky-blue pool with a rock waterfall. His Clarita and her husband owned this house. Those Miami Cubans would be impressed. It had all been worth it. The risk he and Violeta took, the hardship of starting over, the years of work.

"Papi? Is that you?" Clarita called from the kitchen.

"Sí, ya voy," Alberto answered.

Clarita, her freshly-dyed auburn hair held up in a messy knot by a plastic clip, wiped her hands on a stained, white apron. She reminded him so much of Violeta. The kitchen smelled of garlicky roast pork. His daughter spooned yellow deviled-egg filling into a plastic baggie. She squeezed the filling together, pressing the baggie, and snipped a corner tip with scissors.

"Where is everybody?" Alberto asked.

"Rogelio just finished mowing. He's in the shower."

Clarita squeezed the baggie, funneling swirls of yellow into the hard-boiled egg halves neatly arranged on a platter. "And Albertico was wiping off the patio furniture. I said he should take a quick swim when he's done. Pobrecito, I think he's nervous. Yadira called. They're a good two hours away. They'll be here twelve, twelve-thirty."

"Here is dessert, hija." Alberto placed the box and bottles on the kitchen island. "I'm going to visit with my grandson." He took an egg from the platter and popped it whole in his mouth.

"They're not ready," Clarita said.

"I'm a growing boy," Alberto mumbled through his mouthful.

The Florida sky was as clear and blue as the pool. Alberto grew basil, oregano, and rosemary in large terracotta pots strategically placed around the lanai to catch the sun. He snapped a sprig of basil, breathed its scent, and stuck it behind his ear—a childhood habit—basil to keep the island gnats and flies away from his face when he played.

"Albertico? Are you out here?"

"S'up, Abuelo?" his grandson said, coming out of the pool-bath.

"Looks like we have everything ready for your young lady."

"Yeah, I see Mami's gone all Martha Stewart. Did you see the new towels *and* fresh flowers in there?" Albertico tilted his head toward the bathroom.

"She wants what is best for you, mijo. A good impression. We have never met these people, alabao' mijo, we have only met Yadira once, and only visited for moments. You two drove down for that party your friend gave. What is his name? I can never remember. Anyway, poof, you were in one door and out the other. We hardly saw you."

Albertico had brought Yadira home for a weekend. He'd told his mother he'd met a girl, and were Facebook official. Alberto had shaken his head. In Cuba, official meant the man went to the girl's father, asked permission to see her, and then visited the home in the evenings or went out with the girl's mother in tow. Now official meant you clicked something on the computer. By the time his Clarita became a young lady, he and Violeta had lived in Coquina Shores for over fifteen years, and they knew the American ways. They were fortunate.

Clarita caught Rogelio's eye, or was it the other way around? Rogelio's people were Cuban refugees, too. The families knew each other. Alberto and Violeta permitted Clarita to go out unchaperoned, but there had been some of the traditional formality. Rogelio had spoken to Alberto first. Now here was his grandson serious about a girl, and the families had yet to meet.

Not that he was really complaining about anything. Things change all the time, whether you have to flee your country or not. He had no regrets. He'd made a good life for himself and his family. In his heart of hearts he knew he'd lived a better life here than in Cuba, even if the revolution hadn't come. He had been a harbor pilot. No special schooling. He'd learned from his father; sailing was a family trade. In the waters around his town, he knew the currents, and the tides. He knew the rocks and the shallows like the palm of his hand. He could bring in to port or take out to open water safely any ship on a moonless night. Knowing the waters got him and his father in and out of the harbor, and a modest life to go with it. That was all. He wasn't one of those foolish old viejos thinking everything in Cuba was sweeter, brighter, better. Qué carajo, and the ones that went back for visits and returned all shocked because their towns weren't the same. What did they expect? Was Coquina Shores, or any part of Florida for that matter, the same as it was fifty years ago?

He did have waves of nostalgia more often these days. But

it wasn't just missing Cuba. It was missing Violeta and their life together. It was missing his younger self—the self that was so busy working a full day he had no time for nostalgia—the self that could take his boat out and spend an entire Saturday or Sunday fishing the Gulf. Some nights, he actually scolded himself into being grateful, because too often instead of thinking this was one day more, he thought, it's just one day less.

Alberto sat in a lanai chair and Albertico sat near him at the edge of the pool, his feet dangling in the water.

"Pués mijo," Alberto said. "You have been un picaflor, a hummingbird tasting one flower after another. Now you have found the perfect flower—Yadira is beautiful and smart."

"Yeah, and she's Latina, too, so when you start with your poetic BS or Mami gets all majadera calling about did I eat and when and what, I don't have to explain anything. She gets it. And, I bet you were a picaflor yourself. Huh? Bet you were, Abuelo." Albertico slid into the water causing ripples across the pool. "Did you buzz-buzz all over those little Cuban florecitas?"

"Only until I found your grandmother."

"So, that's a yes. What's your number, Abuelo? How many flowers we talking about?"

"A gentleman does not tell."

Albertico backstroked away from him singing, "Abuelo was a player. Abuelo was a player. Flor-flor-pica-pica-flor."

Alberto laughed. "That's disrespect. Nothing but disrespect."

By the time the doorbell rang shortly after noon Alberto had changed into a crisp, fresh guayabera. His son-in-law and grandson wore neat and casual shorts and shirts. Clarita had transformed herself from kitchen cook to hostess—auburn hair past her shoulders, carefully applied red lipstick, stylish but simple clothes, half a dozen thin gold bangles jingling at her wrist. He'd given Violeta those gold bangles. He wished she were here, too.

"They're here," his daughter said. "Albertico, Rogelio, Papi, quick, they're here, quick."

"Chill out, Mami!" Albertico said. "I got this."

Everyone gathered at the foyer, and Alberto hung back. This is their time, he thought, and watched his grandson open the door.

Yadira came in first. Young, thick black hair, almond eyes; she greeted Albertico with a quick, shy kiss. Behind Yadira was an older version with the same almond eyes but short hair. Alberto stood back watching as the mothers greeted and hugged, each paying the other mutual compliments on what a lovely child they'd raised. The fathers shook hands and patted shoulders.

"This is Alberto, my father," Clarita said.

"Mucho gusto, bien venidos, it is a pleasure." Alberto covered each hand in turn with both of his.

"And here is mine," Yadira's mother said. "Papi, ven, ven, come all the way in. Yadira, help him, give him room. This is Octavio, mi papá."

Alberto stepped forward to shake the frail old man's hand. He reached out then dropped his extended hand. He stood still and blinked hard one, twice. The third blink brought recognition. He couldn't breathe, his chest hurt, a rising pressure filled his ears. Alberto opened his mouth and what came out was a pained wail. He swung back and slapped Octavio with open palm, hitting his ear.

The impact knocked the old man to the floor.

"Majua!" Alberto screamed and tried to swing again, but someone was holding him back. "Son of a bitch, cabrón. Let me go!"

Alberto tried to break away, but his son-in-law held him tightly from behind, his arms pinned at his side. "Viejo! Old man, what? Viejo, stop." He heard Rogelio say. Alberto saw his grandson cradle the man they called Octavio on the floor. Women shouted. A child cried. Alberto turned around.

Yadira was crying. "What's happening? I don't understand what's happening?"

"Señor Alberto, this is my grandfather. His name is Octavio."

"He is Majua to me."

Clarita was pale. "Papi, you're confused, Papi. It can't be."

He shook his head. "No, my daughter, I am not confused."

"Mami, what the hell is going on?" Albertico asked.

"Señor Alberto, who, what is Majua?" Yadira asked.

"Una majua," Alberto said, "is a small, insignificant little fish."

They had been young boys together, Alberto and Octavio, running barefoot through the dirt roads of their neighborhood. They were friends before first grade and inseparable for the next eight years. Alberto and his family had a two-bedroom cement block house with a tin roof and a pump for water. Octavio's home was even more modest. He lived with his mother and fisherman father in a thatched roof house near the beach. His mother cooked in an outdoor kitchen over a charcoal fire. Octavio's father brought home buckets of majuas—tiny, smelt-like fish often too small to clean. His mother dropped them in a vat of hot oil and Alberto and Octavio ate them, salty and greasy like popcorn. Once, when they were four or five years old, they'd challenged each other to a majua-eating contest. Octavio's mother dropped piles of crispy fish on the paper bag-covered table and they ate, giggling, grease dripping down their bare, thin, sun-browned chests. Octavio won, proclaiming himself the majua champion.

"You *are* a majua," Alberto teased, and his nickname for his friend was born.

After the compulsory eighth grade, Alberto manned the pilot boat with his father and Majua fished with his. They stayed friends, years passed, times changed.

Majua became part of the revolutionary movement. He joined the Comité de la Defensa de la Revolución. Ostensibly a group formed to maintain civil order, it became a watch-dog group. Alberto watched as the subtle power the organization granted Majua began to change him. Small privileges became morsels that increased Majua's hunger for more. Alberto saw this and distanced himself. He was gusano, a worm, not a member of the Party and quietly proud of it.

Alberto took over harbor pilot duties after his father's death. No one questioned his expertise on the waters. But he hadn't joined el Partido Comunista. Alberto's trips in and out of the harbor were monitored. The Bay of Pigs came, and after that disaster, Clarita was born. She was a frail child with food allergies and a tender constitution. The embargo had brought scarcity and rationing of all goods. Finding the right foods for her daughter kept Violeta busy, stressed and afraid.

By her second birthday, Clarita was too weak, too thin, and too small for her age. Alberto and Violeta realized that if something didn't change, Clarita wouldn't see three. They talked, and considered, and vacillated, and finally decided. They had to leave. He and Violeta planned and waited for a moonless night. Alberto prayed for calm seas. He couldn't risk taking the pilot boat, but he owned a motored skiff. He hid it in a secluded cove bordered by sea cliffs and prepared to depart. They took nothing but gas, water, sugar to mix in the child's bottle, and one bag of clothes. Keeping the cargo weight as light as possible provided speed.

Alberto knew the waters, he knew the sentry look-out positions, and he knew the risks.

When the right evening came, Violeta gave Clarita a draught she'd gotten from a curandera to make the child sleep. Alberto would paddle away from the coast, as far as possible, before he started the motor, reducing the risk of being heard. He could make Key West within a day.

Before getting in the skiff, Violeta tied Clarita to her bosom with a blanket. As Alberto wrapped a life jacket around his wife, he whispered, "If you have any doubts, my love, we can turn back."

Violeta kissed his cheek, kissed the top of Clarita's head, and said, "We go now. Together."

Alberto pushed the skiff out until he was thigh-high in water, and climbed in. He paddled, hard. Once he rounded the point on the far side of the cove, water currents changed, and he would start the motor. But as he reached the point, he heard voices. He signaled for Violeta to crouch down. He paddled harder, but the waves pushed them back toward the rocks at the shore. Alberto was surprised. He'd chosen the spot because it was an area that wasn't usually patrolled.

"I can't believe they gave us flashlights to keep. They're Russian. Come up here. Where are you?"

Alberto heard the voice and then saw beams of light dance

across the water. He prayed. He tried to keep the boat still. He kept his eyes on the flashlight beam coming from above them.

"Wait, chico, I'm peeing down here."

The second voice. Alberto knew that voice; he'd grown up with it. A wave pushed the skiff closer to the rocks, and Alberto saw Majua. And Majua saw him, too. Alberto touched his finger to his lips, signaling quiet. He held his hands together in prayer and held them out to his friend. He repeated his motions: quiet, prayer, a silent please. Didn't Majua see him pleading?

"Aquí, down here, aquí!" Majua shouted. "They're trying to get away!"

The flashlight beam quickly scanned the water. Alberto started the motor and pointed the skiff out of the cove. Whoever had the flashlight also had a rifle. A shot hit the water, barely missing the boat.

Violeta screamed.

"Stay down, stay down, stay down," Alberto shouted at his wife. He heard a second shot. The third he heard and felt instantly in his thigh. Alberto kept going. Time and speed were imperative. He knew that by the time Majua and the shooter walked back to town and notified a patrol boat, he needed to be in open water where catching the right currents in the Straits would propel them north, and away. He hoped their head start was enough to facilitate their escape.

He didn't tell Violeta he was hit until he could no longer stand the pain. By then, the lights from the coast were no longer visible. In the weak light of his own small flashlight, Violeta used his belt and Clarita's cloth diapers to apply pressure to his leg.

Sometime in the early morning, in the middle of the Straits, they spotted a U.S. Coast Guard plane. Violeta, with their child tied to her body, stood and waved an orange and black distress flag, rocking the skiff back and forth with her motion. Alberto could not stand.

Alberto sat by the pool, took off his captain's hat, and rubbed it against his thigh. Through the glass doors he saw his family and Majua's all talking at the same time. Yadira held an ice pack to her grandfather's head. Clarita talked, gesturing wildly with her hands, and crying. Majua shook his head. Alberto caught Majua's eyes. Then, Alberto saw him nod, drop his head and cover his face with gnarled hands. That's when Majua's daughter began to cry, too. She hadn't known, Alberto realized, Majua's daughter had never known about any of it. And why would she? Why would Majua speak of such a thing?

Alberto turned away and said in a hush, "Ay, Violeta, the things of this life."

"Abuelo? You okay?"

Alberto shifted around. His grandson had opened the sliding

glass doors just enough to squeeze his body through. The boy sat with him.

"Abuelo, I didn't know. I mean, I knew you'd escaped when Mami was little, and you'd been shot, but I didn't know, you know? The names? I didn't know the real names. And Yadira, she has her father's last name anyway, and she didn't know anything about anything. I swear."

"Basta, mijo, I know."

"I mean you and Abuela, you helped raise me. I would never do anything to hurt you. And," Albertico stood up, kicked his chair. "What a fucking mess. I mean, Jesus, *what* are the goddamn odds?"

"I know, mijo, life is strange."

"Family first. That's what you taught me. I mean, you and Abuela were willing to die for Mami when she was a baby. And, so, I'll do what has to be done." Albertico said hoarsely, "I'll break it off, Abuelo."

Alberto felt his eyes well up. "My grandson is a man of honor."

He looked past Albertico inside the house. Lovely, petite Yadira stood off to the side. He saw her look from her mother tending to her grandfather, to Albertico tending to him, and back. How long did brittle, shrunken Majua have on this Earth? How long did he? Alberto knew that if his grandson lived to be his age, a piece of his heart would always hurt for Yadira.

Albert pushed back his thin hair and put on his captain's hat.

"I am very proud of you, my son. You do not have to choose. I choose for you."

THE LAST LOCK

THE GUARD STOOD AT THE KITCHEN counter, breaking apart
cloves of garlic. Ernesto watched as she lined them up in a straight
line like soldiers. She picked up a broad knife, placed it flat over the
first clove, and smashed it with her fist, crushing the innards. Then
she squashed the next one. Ernesto jumped a little each time. She
scooped up the pulp with the blade and dropped it in a pot. He'd
observed her carefully when she came in tonight—watched her
lock the thick door, and put the keys in the back of a drawer where
she worked. She was new, but there was something familiar about
her. Ernesto watched her silently.

The smell of garlic reminded him of watching Regla cook when
he was a child. He'd cross the breezeway that separated the main
house from the kitchen to join her. He never felt lonely when he
was in Regla's kitchen. Ernesto thought the warm, square room was
more alive than the rest of the house even though they were the
only two there. Regla was tall and lean; her tidy hair always held

up by a white scarf. Ernesto can't remember a day of his childhood without her cooking a meal for him. *You've been eating my food since you were in your mother's womb.* Sometimes she said it as an endearment, sometimes as a scold. She always had something bubbling, simmering, or steaming on the large black stove that owned the wall to the left of the entrance door. On the right wall, he remembered, were shelves. On the top one sat a circular, oscillating fan, on the bottom one a radio; both were always on. The fan cooled the room and spread the smells of onions, roasted meats, fried fish, egg-y flans and custards. On the radio, Regla listened to las novelas—stories of love and bravery—or to music. When she wasn't singing along to songs, she was whistling to melodies.

She had taught him to whistle.

Whistling had kept him sane when he was in solitary. He'd paced the four-foot length of his cell back and forth until he made himself dizzy. He stared at the blank gray walls, discovering that if he stared without blinking, his vision blurred, and his mind projected scenes—the Calle Central of his town, the shore of his favorite beach, and the kitchen of his childhood home—he saw himself young, and safe, and never hungry. Then he whistled "El Manicero," "Guantanamera," all the Benny Moré songs that came to mind, and anything else he could remember—tune after tune after tune until his lips were parched and cracked, and his cheeks ached.

The guard placed a plate with a plump chicken thigh and a serving of yellow rice before him. "Eat."

He was hungry, and it smelled like Regla's cooking, but he pushed it away.

"Look," she said. "Está bien." She picked up a knife and fork, cut a small piece of the chicken, and scooped up some rice.

He watched her chew and swallow.

"It's safe. It won't hurt you."

He couldn't remember the last time he'd eaten, but he'd learned to be cautious. Two, three times, his plate of rice and beans had been tainted with laxatives—enough laxatives to leave him writhing in pain on the floor of his cell, unable to control his bowels, no toilet, no one responding to his pleas for help, soiling himself, left with his own unbearable mess and stench for days.

Ernesto followed the guard's example; he, too, cut a small piece of chicken and scooped a bit of rice. His hand trembled from a combination of age and fear as he brought it to his mouth.

"Do you like it?" she asked.

Ernesto nodded. He chewed slowly and took another forkful.

"It's your favorite. Just like Regla used to make it."

Ernesto dropped his fork. "How do you know about Regla? Do you have her here, too?"

"No. Regla has been gone a long time now."

"Then Regla is safe," Ernesto said.

The woman poured him a glass of water. "Regla has been gone for a very long time, and you're safe. Look, your water is also safe." She took a sip of water. "Now, drink."

Regla was gone. Had they arrested her when they arrested him? He couldn't remember. He couldn't remember if she had been at the house when they came for him. They'd burst in with rifles, the militiamen in their green fatigues. One hit him on the temple with a rifle butt when he tried to shield Eugenia. Where was Eugenia? His beautiful Eugenia.

She hadn't been to visit in a long time.

"My wife's name is Eugenia," he said. "They must be prohibiting her from seeing me."

The guard smiled and said nothing.

"Maybe she's had trouble with transportation. The buses don't run the way they used to from our town to La Habana. Las Palmeras. Do you know it? It's right on the coast." Ernesto carefully cut a piece of meat away from the bone, and ate it. "That's where I first met my Eugenia—by the water." He reached for his glass and drank.

He'd gone with his friend, Benito, to the boardwalk that curved along one side of the bay. Fried fish and cold beer—that's what they'd wanted that Saturday. He'd worn a crisp white linen guay-abera Regla had ironed for him that morning. It smelled of starch. Benito wanted to eat at El Paraíso Verde because he liked the out-side tables with green canvas umbrellas. Besides, they had the best fried grouper in town. They'd sat down and ordered beers, when Eugenia and two other women—one young and one old—sat at the next table. The old one was Doña Amparo, the dentist's wife. He and Benito greeted her cordially, commenting on the pleasantness of the day. Doña Amparo introduced her nieces, visiting from the mountains, she said. Eugenia and her sister planned on spending the entire summer with her, enjoying the salty sea air. He remembered how Doña Amparo's voice had said *aire salubre*, as if she'd been waiting, practicing for just the exact moment to let the words fly from her lips, like flower petals cast to float in the breeze.

Eugenia wore a yellow dress and a white straw hat trimmed with a ribbon of the same yellow. She looked like a daisy, Ernesto thought. A perfect, beautiful, happy daisy.

He asked for Eugenia's hand in marriage at the end of the summer. It was 1955. Two years later, his daughter Eugenita was born.

"I have a daughter," he told the guard. "She was seven when I was arrested. She comes to visit me with her mother. She's a good girl. Eugenia says she is a big help, standing in the lines when the rations come. Eugenia is thin. I don't think she's eating enough. I think she saves her rations to bring to me." Ernesto dropped his fork. "Did Eugenia bring this chicken? I ate it all. Poor thing is probably going hungry, and look what I did?" Ernesto covered his mouth with his hands. "I ate my family's chicken. I ate my family's chicken."

"No, no. I brought the chicken. I came in with it. Remember? I brought it in a bag."

"You came in with a bag."

"That's right. I had the chicken in the bag."

"When you killed the garlic?"

"What?"

"With your knife. Like this." Ernesto pounded the table with his fist.

"Crushed. I crushed the garlic. I didn't *kill* it."

"They were going to kill me," Ernesto said. "The milicianos. When they took me. They wanted to know where Benito was. You see," Ernesto whispered, "I can tell you now because I know he's dead. I know because Eugenia told me. They wanted to know where Benito was. If they could find Benito, they could find the rest of the group. Benito was involved with a group of counter-revolutionaries." Ernesto brought a finger to his lips, letting her know they had to be quiet. "He wanted me to work with him. But I was afraid. Not for me." He sat up straight and pounded his chest with his palm. "For my family, of course, for my wife and my daughter. He was my best friend. They didn't believe me. They didn't believe I didn't know where Benito was. They covered my eyes like this." He placed his napkin over his face. "They ask me again, 'Dónde está Benito?' Again, I say, 'I don't know.' I hear them say: 'Aim!' I hear the rifles cock. I brace myself. I hear: 'Fire!' The bullets don't hit me, but I fall to the ground anyway. The soldiers, they just laughed. The one in charge tells them to put me in a cell to think, because the next time, they won't shoot the bullets over my head. That was my first time in solitary."

"Let's not talk about that anymore. That was a long time ago. Finish eating."

"We have to talk about it. You have to know because—"

"I already know."

"You have to know, because, I see. I see you bring me good food, therefore, you must be a good person in your heart. You have to be careful. You can be innocent, like me, and still be locked up. The way I am, for no reason. There is no justice. Do you believe in justice?"

"I try to believe in justice."

"Then, please, you must let me out. Do what is in your heart. Think of my daughter, my Eugenita. Imagine the struggles of my wife. I ask for them, not for me. The soldiers took my freedom. They took my right as a man. What kind of man can't take care of his family? What kind of man leaves them unprotected? They try to crush me." Ernesto pounded the counter with his fist. "Out! Let me out! Let me out!" He pounded the counter harder and harder.

"Viejo, stop! Stop. You're getting agitated. Vamos, stop. Come, Papi, ven, come sit over here. I'll turn music on. How about the boleros, eh? The boleros are soothing. You like the love songs. Right, Papi?"

"Eugenita?"

"Sí, Papi. Eugenita. We'll go out tomorrow. The weather wasn't good today, but tomorrow, there's no rain. I'll take you out. Do you want to drive to Clearwater? We can walk the beach. You always like the beach."

"Eugenita?"

"Sí, Papi."

A thump awakened Eugenita—a soggy tree limb falling on the roof—it had rained all day, and yesterday, and the day before. The summer rainstorm had left the neighborhood littered with oak and pine twigs, small branches, strands of Spanish moss. She'd dozed off reading the closed captions on the TV while Benny Moré songs played in the background. The music calmed her father, but she'd grown sick of it; the same old songs over and over again. It played at a doctor's office level, just loud enough to silence the silence. Eugenita uncoiled herself from the corner of the couch, placed her feet on the carpet and sat up. Her vision suddenly went dark and cleared up just as quickly. When the head-rush passed, Eugenita rubbed her temples. She was exhausted.

Bad-weather days were the worst. On days when she could take her father out of the house, even if only for a short time, he was calmer. Where to take him was becoming more of a problem. Interacting with non-Spanish speakers frustrated him. Her father had lost his ability to speak English, word by word. He used to enjoy walking around the mall, window-shopping, stopping for coffee or a smoothie, but now the crowds made him anxious and nervous. Parks were fine, but only during school hours when they tended to be mostly empty. Her father was comfortable as long as there weren't too many children playing sports, laughing, or squealing. She'd learned from experience that she could always take him two places: the beach, because even when crowded, he became mesmerized gazing at the water, and the cemetery, with its stillness that prompted visitors to whisper. But, while the cemetery brought her father serenity, it made her melancholy.

His mind had been slowly deteriorating for several years, but it had taken a precipitous downward spiral fifteen months back with her mother's death. She had been his grounding force; the anchor that kept his anxiety at bay when he forgot things, confused people, and finally, became unable to venture out alone because he got lost.

Her mother, mi bella Eugenia, as he called her even on the rare occasions when they argued, had always been the stabilizing presence in her father's life. It was she who had kept him alive during the six years he'd been unjustly imprisoned in Cuba, never missing a visitation, bringing him supplies even if they had to do without at home; it was she who, as if by the sheer force of her presence, imbued him with the spirit to survive. After those six long years, when he was released, thin and hollow-eyed, it was her mother who calmed his sweaty, screaming nightmares with cool towels and herbal teas. And it was her mother who hustled, scrambled, bribed, and made sure that in 1980, when hundreds of boats departed Mariel, they were on one.

Eugenita turned off the television and made herself get up to check on her father. Days like today, when he was particularly distressed and his mind lost its weak grip on reality, exhausted him. They exhausted her, too. At first, she'd tried to correct him, bring him back to the present, attempting to keep him grounded. But often that distressed him further, and it taxed her patience and her nerves. Sometimes she wished his brain worked like the old radios— when they failed to tune in to the correct frequency, a couple of whacks on the side tended to do the trick. Not that she ever wanted to hit her father. Coño, obviously—just that maybe a small whack that took him back to reality would be a blessing compared to the countless times she listened to his repeated stories, or the countless times she repeated herself trying to bring him back.

In the dim living room, Eugenita picked up the newspaper that had fallen from the couch to the carpet, folded the green throw she'd wrapped around her shoulders, and turned off the music. She made her way upstairs, in the narrow house where she'd lived for most of her adult life. She'd moved back in three years ago to help when her mother became ill. It was time. Her mother had asked repeatedly, when she was strong and healthy, not because she'd wanted Eugenita's help, but because she wanted to help Eugenita.

Years ago, on a Sunday afternoon, while on their way to catch a movie matinee, Eugenita and her husband, Paul, had been plowed into on the driver's side by a pickup truck that ran a red light. Eugenita walked away with broken bones: three ribs, a clavicle, and an arm that still bothered her on damp days like today. Paul hadn't walked away at all. Against her parents' urgings, Eugenita continued to live alone in the home she'd shared with her husband. She'd married late—very late, according to her culture. She had been well into her thirties when she'd met her shy husband at an evening computer class at the community college. Eugenita was shy, too, especially around men. She was twenty-three when she arrived from Cuba. She'd found the pace of her new country fast—everything was fast—fast food, fast traffic, fast checkout. At the time, she couldn't comprehend why everyone was in such a hurry any more than she could understand the language. Paul was soft-spoken, and gentle. He liked the way she made café con leche in a pot on the stove, heating the milk slowly so it wouldn't boil over before adding the steaming dark coffee. He liked that she was a helpful daughter who still lived at home with her parents.

After her bones healed, Eugenita returned to her job, and eventually learned that what people said was true—that crushing grief ebbs to a dull ache. She established a peaceful routine that worked for her quiet ways, surrounded by the memories of her husband. She continued to sleep in the bed where he'd taught her how to make love, and to shower in the bathroom they'd wallpapered together.

All the lights were on upstairs. It was her father's habit; he'd come to hate the dark. At the top of the landing, Eugenita toggled down the dimmer switch she'd installed to provide her father with sufficient light if he awoke in the middle of the night. She'd done the same in her parents' bedroom. She entered it now, automatically reaching for the light switch, and was stunned to find her father's bed empty and unslept in.

"Papi!" Eugenita rushed to the bathroom adjacent to the master bedroom. Like the bedroom, its lights were on, but it was empty.

Calling for her father, she checked her own room, and the third one: the combination guest bedroom, sewing room, and office that stored suitcases, the vacuum cleaner, and an ironing board.

Eugenita headed downstairs, calling for her father. The front door was still locked. She went to the side door that led from the kitchen to the carport and to the backyard. It, too, was locked. She rattled the door, muttering, no, no, no. She'd had interior/exterior, key-locking bolts installed months ago, the second time her father wandered out alone and got lost. The first time, he'd left the house midday while she'd been preoccupied at the computer. A neighbor, two streets down, had found him and walked him back before she'd even realized he was gone. The second time was at early evening, when she'd gone in for a shower after dinner, and came out to find him missing. She'd circled the neighborhood in her car and found him a few streets away.

Eugenita went to the kitchen drawer where she kept the key, and it was gone, as she suspected. She thought she'd been careful. She hadn't realized he'd seen her hide it. She kept it there for easy access, for herself and for Arnold, the home care assistant who came for a couple of hours every day to help her father shave and bathe, and to watch him when she needed to do errands around town. Running upstairs to retrieve the duplicate key she kept in her nightstand, Eugenita didn't know what surprised her more: that her father had paid attention to her stowing the key, or that he'd remembered it after the fact.

The wet roads glistened under the streetlights as Eugenita drove slowly around the neighborhood. From the open car window, she called for her father as if calling for a lost pet. Silently she prayed to find him okay. How far could he have gone? How long *had* he been gone? How long had she been asleep? Damn it. The last three days he'd been worse. When he started rambling about his youth, she marveled at the details that he remembered. And when his mind drifted to his imprisoned years, his fear and despair were palpable. Paranoia and fear of persecution came with the dementia, but that was amplified by her father's history. The horrors he'd endured were real. Now, he insisted on keeping the living room window curtains, which opened to the front lawn, closed at all times, and peered through the edges of the drawn curtains routinely to make sure no one was watching the house. If he heard people talking on the front sidewalk or on the street, he was certain they were looking for him. Her father kept a small duffle bag in his closet packed with a change of clothes, a flashlight, matches, and cans of Libby's Vienna Sausages—survival essentials.

After one cruise around the neighborhood proved fruit-less, Eugenita decided that if she didn't find him after one more go-around, she'd call the police. She hated to do that. Uniforms terrified him now. When a bank security officer had opened the door for them recently, she'd seen her father cower in fear.

"Where are you? Where are you?" Eugenita whispered between loud calls of "Papi!"

On impulse and out of desperation, she called Arnold. Ten months ago, he'd been a godsend. He was strong enough to be forceful, and gentle enough to appease her father's anxiety. Arnold, born to a Cuban mother and a Puerto Rican father, also spoke the right dialect to coax her father into doing what he needed.

"Papi, stay still so I can trim those nails of yours. What? You planning on digging boniatos for dinner with them? Vamos, chico, chin-chan, and I finish."

"I told you," Arnold said. "I told you he's much worse."

"It's the rain."

"Ay, mija, it is not just rain, chica. Seriously, he needs to be in a facility full time. His doctors told you. I told you. And why do you think? Because I like talking myself out of a good gig? Por Dios."

A faint cry escaped Eugenita.

"Okay, chica, never mind now. Look, you keep driving around. We know he'll do better if you find him. Keep calling out for him, but call the police. I'll head for the house in case he comes back. I can be there in fifteen."

Eugenita called 9-1-1 as Arnold insisted. Then, she drove the neighborhood again, going up and down each street slowly. She ventured farther, to the park adjacent to the nearby elementary school, where they sometimes went for walks. Nothing. By now he could be anywhere. She circled back around.

This was her fault. Arnold was right. The doctors had said months ago it was time for a full-time care facility. She hadn't wanted to do that to her father. She hadn't wanted to hand him over to the care of strangers. But was what she was doing any kinder? Keeping him locked in his own home? If she was honest with herself, she had to question if she was doing this for her father or for herself.

Eugenita started when her cell phone rang. Two police officers in a cruiser had spotted her father about two miles away from her house. He was unhurt but distraught. They didn't want to force him into the cruiser. Did he speak English? He didn't seem to understand.

When Eugenita approached them, she saw the police car with its lights on, and her father sitting on the sidewalk curb, clutching his duffle bag.

Her father stood up when he saw her. "Eugenia! Run! I escaped and they found me. Run! They will arrest you, too."

Eugenita decided the fastest way to calm him was to follow his lead. "It's okay, Ernesto. They're friends. Counter-revolutionaries in disguise. On a secret mission," she whispered in Spanish. "And they're going to let you come with me."

Eugenita took her father by the elbow. She showed her identification to the officers. Yes, her father had spoken English at one time, but now it was all gone. No, taking him to the hospital tonight wasn't necessary. Yes, she had the name of his doctor for the report. Yes, she was looking into full-care facilities. Yes, a social worker could follow up with her. Whatever was necessary. The important thing was to get him home. His pants were wet from sitting on the ground. His shoes were soaked from walking through puddles.

Arnold was waiting at the house when they returned. He helped Eugenita get her father cleaned up and ready for bed.

"My wife is very brave," her father told Arnold as they got him into bed. "She saved me from the milicianos."

"Yes," Arnold said. He pulled a blanket from the foot of the bed over her father's legs, up to his chest, and then, as if crimping dough around the rim of a pie, he tucked the fleece snugly beneath the outline of his body. "Sleep, now."

Eugenita nodded agreement and patted her father's head. "That's right, sleep now. You're safe." She turned off the lamp on the nightstand.

"Don't turn off the lights," her father said.

"No, not all. I'll just turn them down a little, just enough to help you sleep."

Eugenita dimmed the overhead lights as she left the bedroom.

Downstairs, Arnold followed Eugenita into the kitchen.

"How about some coffee?" she asked.

"No. It's pretty late. I'd better—"

"Wine? A glass of wine?" Eugenita reached for glasses before Arnold could answer.

He sat at the table in the same spot where, earlier that evening, she'd fed her father.

She poured a couple of inches of wine into a glass and placed it before him. "Thank you, for everything, de veras, Arnold, thank you."

"No sweat, chica. I'm just glad he was found okay. Your father thinks you are your mother. You must be a lot like her to remind him of her this much."

Eugenita didn't respond. She was nothing like her mother. Her mother faced the world head on and did whatever needed to be done. Eugenita had closed herself off after Paul was gone. She'd made her world smaller still when her mother became ill. She'd retired early. Eugenita had felt comfortable in the cocoon of her parents' house. Taking care of one and then the other, she'd convinced herself, was enough. She hadn't kept her father home for him; she'd kept him home for herself.

"I'll start looking into full-care facilities tomorrow," she said to Arnold. "I'll arrange to check them out in person when you're here with him."

When Arnold left, Eugenita locked the door behind him, and put the key in her pocket. In the quiet kitchen, she picked up the empty wine glasses, wondering what and whom she'd remember when she got to be her father's age. A few drops of wine had fallen on the pinewood table. She thought it looked like blood and wiped it off with the palm of her hand. She rubbed one hand with the other, and the trace of wine was gone. Then tears came to her eyes because she knew when her father died, there wouldn't be anyone to remember her.

ACKNOWLEDGMENTS

The primary reason I was able to write these stories, am able to write at all, is because of the courage of my parents, Noel and Aracelis González, to get on a shrimp boat with young children and leave Cuba via the Camarioca Boatlift in 1965. Their sacrifice and struggle have given me an amazing life. To them, my Papi and Mami, I owe everything. And also, to the extended family and community that helped raised me. My Tío Onil who sailed to get us, my Tía Cachita who stayed behind alone in Florida and waited, my Abuela Pura who was my second mother, and the rest of the clan—los González y los Fernández—all the other abuelos, tíos, tías, y amigos de la familia. Listening to them tell stories over tables laden with food, saladitos, and cold beers inspired my desire to capture our history and our culture on the page.

My gratitude to Black Lawrence Press: Diane Goettel, Abayomi Animashaun and the editorial board of the Immigrant Writing

Series for making this book, and my dream, a reality.

My thanks also to:

Susan Hubbard, my first creative writing teacher, who years ago told a forty-something woman afraid to show her work that she had a voice.

Rita Ciresi—teacher, mentor, thesis advisor, and friend—for years of encouragement and support.

John Fleming, Heather Sellers, Helena Viramontes, Laura Pegram, Anjanette Delgado, Ana Menéndez, Luis Alberto Urrea, and Andre Dubus III, whose workshops and editing helped develop these stories.

My fellow classmates at the University of South Florida MFA Program for their camaraderie and insight.

The Bread Loaf Writers' Conference, Writers in Paradise, and the New York State Summer Writers' Institute.

Annie Bronston for years of reading and improving everything I send her, and for her friendship. It was an auspicious day for me when I met Annie, Lisa Holewa, and David Jasper in my first writing class.

My dear writer friends, Jennifer Murphy, Sharon Snow Pinson, and Christine Lasek, mil gracias.

My love and gratitude to the friends and family who are outside of my writing world, but always in my corner:

My brothers, Noel and David González—ay, Dave, how I wish you were here!

Jan De Luz, my Armwood Hermanas, my Lake Magdalene family, Jan Asendorf, and the Tampa Bay Book Group, your friendship, support, and encouragement are gifts.

My children—my everything—I'm so lucky to be your mother. Gracias, Alexa, for being the first reader of these stories, and gracias, Cord, for always cheering me on.

Lastly and always, Alan—my love, my husband, my best friend, my champion, my heart. I'm grateful we had forty years together, but our time was still not long enough. I wish I could show you this book, and I miss you every single day.

Stories in this collection have previously appeared in the following publications:

"The Lost Ones," *Kweli Journal* and the anthology *All About Skin: Short Fiction by Women of Color,* University of Wisconsin Press, ©2014

"For If the Flies," *The Acentos Review*

"Emelina," *The Hong Kong Review*

"Consuelo's Garden," in the anthology *Home in Florida: Latinx Writers and The Literature of Uprootedness,* University Press of Florida, ©2021

"Dressing the Saints," *2 Bridges Review*

"Harbor Pilot," *Litro*

"The Last Lock," *TriQuarterly Review*

"Hector's Woman," *Aster(ix) Journal*

Marion Albanese

ARACELIS GONZÁLEZ ASENDORF was born in Cuba. Her work has appeared in *TriQuarterly*, *Brevity Magazine*, *Kweli Journal*, *Aster(ix) Journal*, *The Adirondack Review*, *Puerto del Sol*, *The South Atlantic Review*, and elsewhere. Her stories have been anthologized in *100% Pure Florida Fiction* (University of Florida Press, 2000), *All About Skin: Short Fiction by Women of Color* (University of Wisconsin Press, 2014), and *Home in Florida: Latinx Writers and the Literature of Uprootedness* (University of Florida Press, 2021). She is the recipient of the 2016 South Atlantic Modern Language Association Graduate Creative Writing Award for Prose, and a 2019 Sterling Watson Fellow. She lives in Tampa, Florida.